To my family in-person and online.

TWO TRUTHS AND A LIE

Lie: I lov<u>ed</u> you.

Truth: I love you. Present tense, or maybe I just love what we had, or could have had, until you went and messed it all up.

Second Truth: I wish things were different. Everything happened so much better in my head. I miss the memories and the daydreams. I miss who I used to be. I miss you, and I miss me, both together, but also separately.

Me. You. Two truths.

Me and you. The lie.

I don't really like to curse but it f*cking hurts.

Call me crazy.

But it f*cking hurts.

Call me stupid.

But it f*cking hurts.

Call me a stupid girl stuck on stupid, meaningless things.

But it f*cking hurts.

CHAPTER ONE: PEAS, PEAS, PEAS, WHERE ARE THE DAMN PEAS?

There is just one thing missing from my life right now. I've been on this earth for eighteen years. I'm two weeks away from being confined to cement walls of a college dormitory three hours away from home. I'm either entering a new phase of life like a reborn star or a mid-life crisis barely halfway through life, and all I want is one lousy can of peas.

Now I know what you're thinking; it's a quarter-life crisis. *Ding. Ding. Ding.* We have a winner in a pair of sweaty gym shorts and dirty sneakers with even dirtier hair. A young adult female standing in the middle of aisle three on the verge of a mental breakdown over a can of peas.

There's canned corn, canned carrots, canned yams, canned string beans, and yet no canned peas. The cans are all a mix of red, whites, and greens. Even with all the different brands, none say the word peas.

"Ow!" My hand flies up to my head. I'd be lying if I said I wasn't disappointed that the culprit isn't a can of peas. I momentarily thought—hoped would be too much—someone saw me in the security cameras and took pity on me. Instead, a box of chocolate cake mix flew over the shelf and ping-ponged its way down. Though, first, it

smacked the top shelf, the top of my head, and the side of my shoulder before now sitting on the floor beside my feet.

I go to sidestep away from the suspicious box as another box comes flying over the shelf and whacks me in the shoulder. I almost want to say something, but I'm still trying to decide if this is real or a quarter-life crisis-induced hallucination. I also can't decide whether to rub my shoulder or my head. I would do both, but I've got a bag of egg noodles in my right hand, and my left hand swipes up the vanilla cake mix off the floor instead.

I glance around, looking for people and cameras. Ideally, John Quinones from *What Would You Do* would pop out. Instead, I get a front-row seat to another red box flying over the shelf. Thankfully, it doesn't hit me this time but instead lands with a resonating thud against the white linoleum floor. The maroon slice of cake on the front says red velvet.

"Dude! Wrong aisle!"

A guy skirts into view at the other end of the aisle—literally—his sneakers squeak like hot rubber tires against the floor. I'm sure they left black scuff marks before he jogs towards me. He's wearing the maroon employee polo and light grey sweatpants. I should turn around. I will myself to turn around and jog away in the opposite direction, but it's too late.

The guy stops in front of me, two cake boxes away. He sucks in a deep breath through his nose, expanding his chest as far as it can go before exhaling and relaxing his stance.

"Sorry about that," he says, bending down to swipe up the red velvet box. "I was restocking the cake mix when my"—he pauses and leans in closer to the shelf— "idiot friend tossed them over the wrong shelf."

A low grumble emits from the shelf, which means his friend heard him.

"It's fine." I chirp as he bends down and picks up the chocolate cake mix, but my body stills again when he straightens back up.

We stand there just staring at each other before he extends his hand out. My eyebrows furrow, but then my brain reminds me I'm still holding the vanilla box. The egg noodles almost slip from my grasp, but I manage to tug both items closer to my chest.

"Oh! I think I'm going to keep this one." Even though it's not on the list my mom gave me, the red spoon on the box signifies it's not any ordinary cake mix, but rather *Betty Crocker* cake mix. Part of me wants to ask if it's on sale, but when I glance back up, his lips are quirked on one side, and my rationality flies over the opposite shelf.

"So, vanilla is your drug of choice." His eyes suddenly feel hotter than the humidity outside. My brain automatically spits out an internal curse, but I quickly shoo it away because I shouldn't care. For a second, I don't care. I went for a run in the summer heat—sue me. Sweaty hair, don't care. Then our eyes lock again, and instead of a box of cake mix, I'm smacked in the face with his grin.

"I'm more of a red velvet kind of guy myself." He holds up the box and gives it a tap with his knuckles. "But if it makes you feel any better, these are on sale today."

Insert drooly face and heart eyes. Clean up on aisle three. Quarter-life crisis girl has melted into a sweaty puddle.

"I'm Trent."

The declaration makes me glance at his shirt, finally noticing the name tag resting there.

Trent is quick to follow my gaze and, as if noticing it

himself, he points to it with a laugh. "And I guess it's right there."

"Yo! I found the microwavable pizza! All we need are some boxes of hot pockets, and our pizza lasagna dreams will be complete." A lanky guy who also happens to be wearing the maroon employee polo throws said frozen pizza box in the air as he saunters down the aisle. When the pizza box lands back in his hands, his eyes land on me. "Oh, why hello there." He sends me a slow, television host-like wink before he straightens his posture. "Have you ever had pizza lasagna?"

I shake my head.

"How about burrito lasagna?"

I shake my head again.

"Hamburger lasagna?"

A laugh escapes me as a dramatic gasp escapes him.

"What are you doing with your life?"

Trent reaches out and shoves his shoulder. "Ignore him."

The kid sidesteps, but his gaze doesn't waver. "You know you look sort of familiar. I think we went to the same high school, no? But you were in the grade below us?"

It would make sense with only about three hundred people per grade that they would recognize me from the halls. I can vaguely picture the lanky guy's flopping brown hair under a beanie of some sort; maybe his name is Jack or Carter or something. Then again, it's only been a few months since I graduated, and I've already put up a mental wall between me and the last four years of my life. Once again, I didn't choose the quarter-life crisis; the quarter-life crisis chose me.

"Two years," Trent says, but then quickly clears his throat. "Stop being creepy."

His friend sticks his tongue out. "It's called being friendly. You should try it sometime."

Trent shoves him again, but this time the skinny kid reciprocates, creating a perpetual cycle of shoulder shoving that only gets more intense as it goes on. I don't know whether to laugh or walk away, but instead, I do neither as my gaze falls.

Trent's sneakers are a mix of grays and have hints of dark blue. One of the dirty white laces is missing an aglet and fraying, flapping up and down as he gets shoved around. The sight makes me internally cringe, and my eyes dart to the cans on the shelf resting beside his feet.

"Peas!" I gasp before practically body slamming the shelf as I reach for the can. Cue the confetti. Pop the champagne. Assistance is no longer needed on aisle three. Quarter-life crisis averted. I'm so giddy it takes me a second to stop my legs from doing what I hoped looked like a happy dance, not a potty dance, and wipe the smile off my face.

Both boys stare back at me as if I just knocked them on the head with a box of cake mix. Trent is quick to shake the expression away with a wrinkle of his nose. His friend's face transforms more slowly from perplexity to a smirk, like the Grinch, as he lifts his elbow up and rests it on Trent's head. Trent quickly shoos him off, leaving them both to start another shoving war with snickers and grunts that remind me of my little sister. This reminds me of my mom, the peas, and the grocery list I still need to complete.

"Well—" I finally step back, making the boys freeze. They attempt to straighten themselves but look more sheepish than composed. "I'm…I'm gonna go." I flick my thumb over my shoulder for emphasis before turning around, ducking my head down, and speed walking away.

"Wait!"

"Ha, too late!"

I ignore them as I turn out of the aisle, taking my peas, egg noodles, vanilla cake mix, and the rest of my dignity with me.

CHAPTER TWO: NOTE TO SELF

Note to self: please don't ever go to the grocery store in running shorts and a t-shirt ever again, especially after going for a run on the hottest day on record so far. This is because there is a point zero one percent chance you will bump into a cute boy in the maroon employee polo, and there is a ninety-nine-point nine percent chance that you'll have sweat stains on your chest, back, and armpits.

There's also a point zero, zero, zero, one percent chance of getting hit by, not one, but two, boxes of cake mix, and even less of a chance of it being because cute boy's friend—who also happens to work there and is also fairly attractive, threw it over the wrong shelf. So, really, it's not my fault. It's theirs. I, on the other hand, really, really, really need to stop thinking about it—especially when I shove my way through the front door with two large reusable shopping bags slung over my shoulders filled with heavy things, like milk, cans, and sour cream.

Another note to self: ignore the devil on your shoulder when it says you can make it inside the house with all the groceries on one trip. Suck it up, take two trips from the car, and save yourself before it's too late.

I drop both bags onto a wooden chair, adding to all the dings these chairs have suffered through over the years. My

mom would have thrown a fit if I dumped them on the kitchen table even though it is already branded with many scruffs and scrapes. Believe it or not but crayons and markers are not as washable as they claim to be, and drawing was always my sister and I's favorite pastime.

"Hey, mom."

She turns from her place at the stove. I finally notice the silver cordless house phone tucked between her ear and shoulder.

"Sorry." I mouth, and she flashes me with a quick smile before going back to nodding along to whoever's on the other end. With all the "uh-huhs" and "yeahs" she keeps humming, it's most likely my grandma. She loves to watch the news, but sometimes she watches a little too much late-night, dateline, real life crime documentaries. I know she'd bottle me up or tuck me inside her purse for safekeeping if she could.

I start pulling stuff out of the bags while my mom lifts the lid off the pan, and I get a whiff of farts, which can only mean she's frying up some broccoli or cauliflower. Sundays are meal prep days since my parents usually work three to five days a week plus overtime and on alternating night shifts. A cop and a nurse, everything rom-coms are made of. It started with coffee and doughnuts, and now it's meal prepping, and a fridge filled with Pyrex.

My mom moves the contents around with a spatula with one hand before coming over to help me.

"What's this?" she whispers, holding up the box of vanilla cake mix.

"It was on sale."

"Yeah, but that's not fair to you…" She grips the phone and heads back to the stove.

I take that as my cue to quickly toss the box into the

cabinet, keep unpacking, and not think about how that box also hit me in the shoulder. I can still feel the thud. I can still hear the smack from when it landed on the floor beside me. I can still hear the words forever echoing inside my head. *'So, vanilla is your drug of choice.'* So creepy out of context but in the moment—

"Thank you." My mom breathes.

I look up from the assortment of cans I was squishing together on the corner of the table. "What?"

"Thank you." She nods towards the table as she walks over and scoops up the two milk cartons, oat for me and almond for Layla. "For getting groceries."

"Oh, no problem." I start laughing a little, at myself mostly, because I keep thinking about getting hit in the head with a box of cake mix—and the fact that I actually got hit in the head with a box of cake mix. "What would you do without me?" I add, like always, but unlike always, my mom freezes and looks up.

It's not the "how-could-you-say-such-a-thing?" kind of look, rather the "I-love-you-so-much-and-am-so-proud-of-you-but-am-going-to-miss-you-like-crazy" kind of expression. I recognize it from the first time I brought my light blue cap and gown home from school, even while it was still in the packaging, and then at graduation. She tried to wave the tears away then to take pictures, but not when I barreled towards her after the ceremony, pushing through the crowd. That look has always been my anchor in life, but especially at that moment when she wrapped me up in a hug. It was one of those "I-never-want-to-let-go-kind-of-moments," but not in the sad sense, rather in the content, "need-to-remember-this-forever-and-ever," kind of way.

We finish putting away the groceries before she shoos me away with a casual flick of her hand—time to shower

and leave her and the fart smell in the kitchen.

"Wait, Lacie."

"Yeah?"

She tilts the phone away from her mouth. "Where are the frozen peas?"

"They had to be frozen?"

My mom nods and turns back to the stove.

I didn't even need to be down the canned food aisle. I didn't need to be standing there for who knows how long panicking because I couldn't find a can of peas. I wouldn't have gotten hit in the head and the shoulder by boxes of cake mix if I had gone to the frozen aisle. I would never have locked eyes with the cute boy who claimed his name was Trent, and his drug of choice was red velvet.

I tentatively reach back up into the highest cabinet and pull down the can of peas. My mom passes me a wary glance before waving me off again, signaling for me to leave the can on the counter.

Now that's my cue.

I run up the stairs, light on my toes out of habit, even though my dad is working overtime at the hospital rather than sleeping off the weekend night shift.

I open my bedroom door to reveal the light lavender walls, and my little sister, Layla, sprawled across the floor with measuring tape.

"What are you doing?" I ask, but she doesn't even flinch. The silence is expected. She's wearing her signature thinking face, furrowed eyebrows and a little piece of tongue poking out of the side of her lips.

I step over her legs and flop down on my bed, or at least try to, on the part not covered by bags. I honestly couldn't even tell you what's in them. I should know. I made a checklist. One minute, I had two months to start packing

up my life, but now I only have two weeks. I'm starting to question why I chose to go away to college in the first place. At least, only point zero, zero, zero one percent. The rest of me is honestly lazy.

I continue to stare up at the ceiling, even when I hear the measuring tape snap shut.

"Your room is eleven point eight inches wider than mine."

"Point eight?"

"Yes, I triple-checked."

I laugh. "Of course, you did. I mean." I sit up and rub my temples. "I know."

"How would you know? You've never measured it before."

"No, I mean, I know you triple-checked."

"Oh." She nods. "You smell like sweat."

I laugh again. "I know."

"And your carpet smells like sweat."

"So does yours."

"No, it doesn't."

"Did you triple-check?"

"What?"

"Nothing." I finally stand up and stretch. The pit stains are still one-hundred percent real and intact. Note to self: heathered grey is not a good color to work out in.

"Bye." Layla exits.

"Bye." I wait a few seconds before following her out only I swerve left to go to the bathroom at the end of the hall, while I know she went right, back to her room.

I plant both hands on the side of the sink and look up into the mirror. I always remember those silly little surveys from grade school, "what's your favorite thing about yourself?" I would always say "my eyes" because they were

just like my grandma's, an olive green. The grandma on my mom's side, not the one on the other side of the phone. The one I never got the chance to meet.

But right now, they look like nothing. I see nothing but the bright green eyes locked with mine in aisle three.

Note to self: nothing will ever compare to that green.

CHAPTER THREE: ICE BREAKING

"Are you sure you have everything?" my mom asks. It's the same question she's been asking me for the last two weeks—heck, the last month—only this time I really take the time to consider the question instead of automatically giving a huffed-out affirmation.

I can say yes if I'm being rational, like the biology major I am. Almost everything I own—and then some—is now stuffed up in dorm room 314 on the third floor of Pemberley Hall. If I'm philosophical, like the core class I have to take this semester that I'm trying hard not to dread, does anyone ever truly have everything?

"I think so." I finally say when I realize my parents haven't stopped staring at me. We're standing in the middle of the sidewalk on the outskirts of one of the many parking lots surrounding the campus.

My mom shrugs her purse higher up on her shoulder and clasps her hands together. "Your toothbrush?"

I nod.

"Toothpaste?"

I nod again.

"Floss? Deodorant?"

"Can we go now?" Layla whines.

"Shower shoes? Because there are so many germs." My

mom continues before her eyes meet mine again. "Towels! How about towels? Do you have enough towels?"

"Maybe we should go buy you some more towels." My dad chimes in, untucking his polo from his khaki shorts. "We'll just head back up the street. I'll check the GPS." He whips out his phone and almost drops the car keys in the process. My parents begin whispering and nodding like they're part of some secret protection program. They both took off to help me move in, but it was more like them moving in and me helping.

"You guys." I laugh. "I think I'm..." My words falter when I'm met with their eyes again. For a second, I'm hesitating along with them. For a second, I want to jump back into the car, buckle myself in, and drive away without turning back, but then I take a deep breath. I say the words that, over the past couple of days, I've been willing myself to believe. "I'm okay."

My mom opens her mouth to say something but then decides against it and clasps her hands in front of her again. "Okay," she says with an affirmative nod. "Okay." She repeats as she waves a hand in front of her face before she pulls me into a hug. We both share an inhale. I specifically inhale the cool powdery scent of her perfume and, essentially, my childhood. "I love you," she whispers into my ear before she turns her head and places a chaste kiss on my temple.

"I love you too," I mumble into her chest before we both pull away, so I can embrace my dad.

"Have fun," he says as he plants a big wet kiss on the top of my head. "But not too much fun." He flicks his sunglasses down. He's no doubt covering whatever possible emotion is clouding over his eyes, making my heart squeeze on the inside, but I laugh on the outside.

"Love you, too."

"Can we go now?" Layla's practically stomping her foot.

"Yes." Mom laughs. "Wait!"

Layla's already diving back into the car and buckling herself back up.

"Aren't you going to say goodbye to your sister?"

I peek in through the cracked window.

Her eyes are already buried in her book. "Bye."

"Bye, Lay," I say, but who knows if she even hears me. She's halfway through *A Walk to Remember* for the thousandth time. She's always reading Nicholas Sparks on an endless loop. She reads one book every month at least three times, and if it has a conjoining film, she'll watch it at least once every week—sometimes more. I'm tempted to reach into the car and shake her yellow, blonde bangs. I've always wanted to move them from the equally parted triangle she makes in the middle of her forehead, but she would kill me. Correction: my parents would probably kill me first, and then, once she was done freaking out, she'd finish the job.

I step back from the curb, and my parents sandwich me in one final hug before they buckle themselves back up in the car. They send me a few waves through the windows. My hair flies around in the shadowed reflection on the back window on the right side. I always get the right, while my sister usually sits on the left. I pull strands out from between lips but can't even bring myself to fully fix the rest of my hair as the black truck pulls away. The lunch we ate a few hours ago, the wrap I could barely even bring myself to eat as I sat there with the three people I always eat most of my meals with, seems to shrivel up inside my stomach. My heart thumps extra hard in my chest, and my fingers clench the strap of my cross-body bag.

I will myself to breathe. I slowly inhale a large breath and let it out. I repeat the process for a second time before I finally turn around and come face to face with the campus I'm now supposed to call home. All the tall brick dorm buildings are outlined by a cement pathway, but they seem like they grew from the grass itself. As if they are as old as all the oak trees but not as tall. The trees stretch higher into the sky. The biology major in me is happy to see nature still standing so strong amongst the concrete. Yet, on the philosophy side, I still can't help but think it's all a little too perfect—not a leaf out of place.

I reach my dorm room and use my student ID to open the door. The bed leaning against the back-right corner is filled with suitcases, totes, and packing boxes. The light blue polka dot sheet looks like it was attempted to be put on before the owner discarded the task.

I was left to take the left side of the room, and it looks like a magazine picture in comparison. My navy-blue comforter is all tucked in with teal, white, and periwinkle flowers imprinted on it. My stuff is already spilling off the small wooden desk. I've got everything from notebooks to toiletries piled up. My laptop tops the pile in its lavender case, and my earbuds dangle on top of it the same way my backpack dangles off the wooden chair. The wood is too bright and too tan to actually be made from the trees outside, but at least we don't have to share one. The only thing we have to share is the tall cupboard-like closet next to the door, but I don't think I'm going to bother. I rather keep my clothes under my bed, in the two trunks we bought last minute, than share a space as small as Layla.

I glance outside the window that divides the room on the back wall. I spot the few people trotting by. The array of cars in the parking lot I trekked over from looks small.

If the people are ants from our third-floor view, the cars are the hills.

I turn back around but find the contents in my stomach churning again because all my stuff is sitting in front of me, yet it no longer feels like mine. I can't bring myself to touch it, let alone move it around or use it.

The door swings open, and a girl walks in. Her dark curly brown hair looks like it embraces the humidity instead of running away from it like mine does. It's also colored with a few light pink and blue highlights. Her fingers tap against her phone screen at lightning speed. She glances up and screams at the sight of me. I scream back. She screams again as if she forgot she already did before silence falls over us again. I'm fidgeting by the window while she continues to stand frozen in the defensive stance she took when she initially laid eyes on me.

She finally throws her head back and laughs, and all the tension uncoils itself from around my spine.

"Sorry." She throws her hands up. "I'm Stephanie. Lacie, right?"

"Yeah." I smile.

Then she's back to tapping away on her phone, and I'm back to teetering in the middle of the room as I try to convince myself to sit on my bed. The silence in the room is only threatened by the echoes of chatter outside our door in the halls.

Stephanie pockets her phone in the back of her jean shorts and stretches her arms into the air. Her long sleeve grey shirt has the university logo splayed across her chest in blue writing. I can't tell if the bold font is tattered and worn on purpose or if it's due to frequent washes. She drops her arms, and her hands slap against her legs.

"Want to go get some food?" Stephanie stares out at

the window behind me as she asks the question, but I still find myself nodding.

"Sure."

I make sure I have my phone and my student ID card in my bag before following her out the door. The dorm room doors are the same orange wood color as all the furniture, but a few of them are already decorated with dry erase and cork boards. I'm too busy attempting to read people's names before I realize Stephanie stopped in her tracks. She pats her back pockets.

"I forgot my ID," she says before she turns and dashes back to the room. She pushes down on the metal handle and shoulders the door before realizing she needs her ID for that, too. She brushes a few wayward curls out of her face and clasps her hands in front of her like a little kid after they accidentally broke something.

I trot back over and slide my ID through, which marks one of the many dashes and rescues that occur for the rest of the weekend. It becomes both a game of who can run, skip, hop, and speed walk to the door first and an inside joke that officially breaks the ice between us.

CHAPTER FOUR: INTRO TO PHILOSOPHY

My alarm went off at six. It's only the second week of classes, but I'm proud because I haven't caved and hit the snooze button yet. Instead, I'm sitting on the floor in between Stephanie's and I's beds stretching my legs.

Stephanie didn't end up making her bed until the first day of classes last week. Even though we tend to have opposite sleep schedules, her hot pink comforter matches mine because there's a big light blue pinwheel of flowers decorating the center. The rest of her stuff also happens to carry a pink and blue color scheme like her hair. From the corkboards she hung over her bed to the makeup she currently has strewn over her desk, it seems like her aesthetic.

Stephanie's curly hair is the only thing I can identify about the lump she's currently making in her bed. I'm glad my early alarm hasn't bothered her yet, or if it has, she hasn't said anything. My first class doesn't start until nine-thirty, but my nerves and fear woke me up the first day— my nerves and fear of the communal bathroom at the end of the hall.

The toilets aren't bad. The stalls are made properly. There is no big underwear exposing crack on the right side of the door when it closes, and I have yet to see any pads

and tampons stuck to the walls. The sinks are all linked together by a single counter and one large mirror.

My fears stem from the showers I have yet to feel comfortable in. I don't care that the water pressure isn't the best or that the tile grout is uneven. What I do care about is that the white curtains resemble the translucent toilet paper hanging in the stalls at the opposite end of the room.

An early morning run helps to get rid of my early morning nerves, while an early morning alarm helps me avoid feeling naked and afraid in front of all the girls on the third floor, their bathrobes, and their beauty products.

I shove my earbuds in my ears as I close the door behind me. The summer humidity is still coating the air when I step outside. The wisps of sunrise poking out of the tops of the dorm buildings make the sky dim and the air cool enough for me to wear leggings, sneakers, and the blue university t-shirt I got at orientation a few weeks ago.

My music blasts in my headphones as I walk to the other end of campus. I go out of my way to avoid the geese poop on the cement pathways but can't avoid the wet morning dew on the grass. The tops of my grey sneakers have a halo of darker material as the water sinks into my cotton socks and chills the tips of my toes.

Once I deem myself far away enough from my dorm building, I turn around and begin jogging back. Sometimes I like hearing each pound of my footsteps. Other times, like today, my music pounds in my ears. Either way, I relish the way my heart pounds inside my chest. It cheers me on, and it's that cheer that propels me through the rest of the day.

I keep my phone in my hand but discreetly pull my student ID out of my bra. Although it's slicked with some

sweat, I didn't trust my hands to keep it from being greased with morning dew somewhere on the grass. I creep into the room the same way the hallway lights do, but luckily, I'm able to close the door and shut them out. Unlucky for a still sleeping Stephanie, my rustling and I can't be shut out.

I gather all my toiletries—towel, shower shoes, an extra towel, shower gel, hair towel, shampoo. The list goes on, but it's all stuffed inside my tote bag. The precarious pile teeters on my bed while I send a text message to Layla.

Have a good day! <3

****

I cringe when the chalk squeaks against the chalkboard. Some guys sitting all the way in the back verbally emit their groans. Professor Collins doesn't even flinch. Instead, he throws us a grin over his shoulder before he finishes writing the word *PLATO* in all caps in the top right corner of the board. It's only been a few classes, but his handwriting gets even more precarious per minute. He's the kind who talks and talks but will stop for questions. He writes down the keywords but doesn't erase the large green chalkboard board until he's filled every nook and cranny with his writing. He'll write diagonal, sideways, and overlap. When he finally erases, he only erases one half of the board at a time. One side of the green board is coated in white powder, while the other half is still coated in words, and he only continues to add more precisely where he sees fit.

He's standing on the small stage like he's been standing there his whole life with a tiny piece of chalk in one hand and nothing but his words waving around in the other. He

doesn't even need a microphone. He projects. He usually wears a pair of slacks and a button-up, but I can picture him and his shiny bald head in an ancient Greek philosopher robe.

"Gazuntite," Professor Collins responds to someone's sneeze before continuing his sentence as if he were never interrupted. My pencil's flying across my notebook at lightning speed, but Professor Collins always talks as if he's making a speech. He goes point by point, piece by piece, and ties it all together with a nice little bow.

We didn't reach the bow-tying today, but another reason Professor Collins gets away with his evil chalk squeaking smiles is that he doesn't mind letting us leave ten to fifteen minutes early.

I flip my notebook closed and push back my chair to grab my backpack. I glance up and catch someone's gaze in the most natural way. The same way a flower stretches its petals to the sun or before two squirrels duel for the same nut. Of course, my biology-oriented brain will conjure up such images in a time like this. Anything to distract myself from thinking the green eyes that meet mine are the same green eyes that met mine in a grocery store a few weeks ago.

I can accept that the Earth's atmosphere is made up of seventy-eight percent nitrogen, yet we, and all the mammals on the planet, are all currently breathing twenty-one percent oxygen. I can accept that oxygen in the air is composed of two oxygen atoms, yet hundreds of miles up, ozone is composed of three. I can even accept that too much oxygen can kill you just as much as not enough oxygen.

But I refuse to believe the random guy, who may not be so random in my hometown, even though I met him at the

grocery store where rom-coms would say "in a meet-cute," is in the same class as me. I know philosophy is all about possibilities, but I'm one hundred percent sure I imagined everything.

****

"Stop!"

"No, you stop!"

"You stop!"

Stephanie came as a package deal. First, there's her older cousin—Savannah. She and Stephanie are sitting on Stephanie's bed with their backs against the wall, laptops on their laps, and their feet dangling off the sides. Stephanie wants Savannah to stop wiggling her feet. Savannah wants Stephanie to stop clicking her nails against her keyboard. Both claim the habit is unavoidable. That's why the silence is interrupted by yelling and shoving every few minutes.

Savannah's black slide on sandal falls on the floor. I guess it lost the competition with the other sandal. A few minutes pass before she flicks her right foot and allows the other sandal to smack against the floor.

"You're so obnoxious," Stephanie mocks but receives another shove to her shoulder. She reciprocates the shove before silence falls over the room again.

In the few days I've known Savannah, I've learned that she's not only a political science major but also that she's on the girls' volleyball team. I've only seen her decked out in school related athletic attire. Her long, black hair is always slicked back in a high ponytail, and her long white socks are always pulled up over her shins or the cuffed ends of her sweatpants.

"I'm thinking about changing my major."

This brings us to Megan, Savannah's roommate, the second part of the package deal. Savannah and Megan are sophomores, and they are the definition of opposites attract.

"Again?" Savannah grunts.

I swivel around in my desk chair to find Megan's seated in a similar position. Her jean-covered legs are crossed and hanging out of the side of Stephanie's wooden desk chair. Her right arm is slung over her notebooks as she bounces the end of her pencil against the paper.

"No, that was my minor. I was considering minoring in philosophy, but now I think I want to major in it instead of psychology."

In the few days I've known Megan, that's probably one of the longest sentences I've heard her say. She's not standoffish. If anything, she's the least intimating out of all four of us with her petite stature, but she always looks so deep in thought. I can never bring myself to interrupt her. Even if she's tapping away on her cellphone, I feel like she's doing something important.

She also is always so put together. Her lips are always glossed, and her light brown hair is always styled and hits below her chin. Stephanie has even called her out on her nonexistent sweatpants a few times, but Megan laughs it off each time and says she feels more comfortable in jeans. I've also been meaning to ask her if she uses a curling iron to get such effortless beach waves in her hair or if it's natural.

"My mom always says if you're considering changing something, that means you should. Otherwise, you never would've considered changing it in the first place." I throw my haphazard advice into the room because ever since

Megan opened her mouth, her eyes haven't left Stephanie's comforter.

"True," Megan mumbles. A beat passes before she turns and flashes me with a small closed-mouth smile.

"What's your major again, blondie?" Savannah asks.

"Biology," I say around my thumbnail.

"Ew." Stephanie shutters. "Science." Her mass of curls is thrown up in a bun on top of her head, and she's got the pajamas to match the evening homework session.

I turn my attention back over to the biology lab in front of me. Week two, energy utilization continues. I purposely left my phone on my pillow to avoid getting distracted. However, a couple of consecutive chimes not only gather my attention, but also the other girls.

"Sounds like someone's popular," Savannah mumbles.

"No." I huff out a laugh. Her tongue is as sharp as Layla's. "It's probably just my sister."

Stephanie shoves her shoulder. "No one asked you, estúpido."

"Look who's talking, fea."

Their bickering ensues while I finally reach to pick my phone up. It probably is Layla and her questions and triple-checked answers. Instead, there are five missed calls from my mom, which alone start to make my hands shake, but there's also only one text from Layla from three hours ago that feels like a bear claw across my chest, raw, ripped, and blistering.

How could you?

We all have our moments when it feels like the world is plotting against us—especially Layla since she's going to be thirteen in December. She's still young enough to be slightly more excused than I am.

Her brain also works differently. It makes her detailed

and straightforward and annoyingly persistent, but in such a confident way I've always envied. Yet sometimes, it makes her seem selfish. Not "act" selfish. There's a difference. She doesn't do it on purpose. It's how her brain works.

It's how it works. It's how it works. "Honey, it's just how her brain works."

I know, I know, I know. "I know, mom, I know."

It still always stings.

"Is everything okay?" Stephanie asks.

"Yeah." I stand back up from my perched position on the end of my bed and begin shoving my feet into my sneakers. "I'll be right back."

"*Ooh*, it must be a lover." Savannah's back at it again. She sends me a wink when I glance back. Stephanie jokingly wiggles her eyebrows, and it only takes a second for Savannah to notice before she shoves her shoulder again.

"Will y'all quit it with the hissy fits," Megan mumbles as she fixes her papers. "Some of us are trying to read."

Savannah and Stephanie share a look before their heads turn to Megan simultaneously. "Y'all!"

Megan shakes her head.

I stuff my ID in my sweatshirt pocket before closing the door behind me.

I trot my way down the three flights of stairs. It will probably take me a couple more weeks before I'm not breathless when I reach the door, but I still push it open. I walk around to the side of the building and stand next to the brick. The orange and pink light from the sunset sears through the clouds. It spills over the tops of the buildings and cuts between the leaves of the tallest trees.

The cement pathways cut through the patches of grass.

Some zigzag while others square around. The brick buildings are all the same faded peach color yet are distinguished by the different names engraved into the cement above the doors. It's all picture-perfect, but it's still not home.

Home is movie nights with my family and too much popcorn. Home is dinner conversations that either end with yelling over who's going to wash the dishes or spit takes and hyena laughter over the impressions my dad does of our grandparents. Home is the blunt words. "Are you going to wake up now?" my sister says every Saturday morning even though she'll probably spend the rest of the day avoiding me.

Home is the first day of school—when you wake up with dread in your bones. You walk into the building with butterflies even though you've been through this same routine since you were five. The humidity sticks to your hair and your skin, but summer is now a distant memory. When you finally come home, you plan to eat a snack, maybe even take a nap, but the second your parents ask how your day was, the dam breaks. Tears stream down your face, and snot drips out of your nose. You can't remember how to breathe.

Your sister is beside you the whole time, or at least always standing there. She may not have the same, red-rimmed eyes and puffy cheeks. She may just stare at you from the hallway as you lay on your bed, staring at the ceiling. Even though she doesn't say it, you know she at least has the same dread for tomorrow that doesn't go away for a few weeks.

But this year I wasn't there when I had to go to my first college class. I couldn't go home to my mom and her reassuring words that usually turn into bone-crushing hugs.

I'm not there right now.

"Lacie?" my mom picks up on the first ring.

"Hey, is everything okay?"

"I'm sorry, I know you're busy with your schoolwork."

"No, it's okay—"

"Get out!" I hear Layla yell.

"But honey." My mom tries, as Dad coos, "sweet pea."

"No! Get out, get out, get out!"

There's some shuffling before there's a soft click of a door.

"You're going to be late," my mom says.

"I know, I know, I'm jumping in the shower." My dad sounds farther away.

"Mom?"

"Yeah, I'm here. Sorry, Lace, your dad and I can't..." My mom sucks in a breath. I wish I could do the same. "She's just laying on your bed, and we can't...We can't get her to get up. I'm pretty sure was up all last night, and she hasn't eaten all day."

My finger traces the line of grout between the bricks. "Put me on speaker."

"Okay." A beat passes before my mom gives me another, quieter, "okay," which means she slid the phone under the door.

I wait another beat for my mom to tiptoe away like I know she will. "Hey, Lay...I'm...here. I know I'm not there, but I'm still...here."

As always, the silence is expected, but it's that damn silence that breaks the dam on my resolve. The barrier I've built since my parents pulled away is breaking—one by one, the water bursts through the cracks. I swallow, but it's no use. I slide my back against the building until I'm crouched on the cement. My head falls between my knees.

I will myself to breathe.

She's probably lying there in the dark with the hood of her favorite blue sweatshirt pulled over her head and her eyes squeezed shut. The hiccups I hear every few seconds mean she's also trying as hard—if not harder—to catch her breath.

My room, once littered with all these things; like piles of clothes on the floor, shoes always creeping out of the closet, and books on shelves I always told myself I'd get around to reading, is now practically drained of any trace of me.

"You left me," she whispers. "Why did you have to leave me?"

"I'm right here." I can barely get the words out because I'm not there. I should be there. I want to be there. I wish I was there, but I'm not.

When we were little, we used to make blanket forts. It was just the two of us crammed underneath kitchen chairs draped with sheets. We always said it was us against the world. Then, one day, the sheet fell on us. I laughed. Layla forgot how to breathe.

It kept happening. Clothes tags, woolen socks, and even the knit blankets that are the last things our mom has left from her mom.

At first, my parents thought it was anxiety. The doctors agreed. We stopped making forts.

She started reading more. She's okay with eye contact. She likes making people uncomfortable by staring them down. She hates math but loves memorization. She likes being social when she wants to be. She likes meeting new people, most of the time. She hates anything neon but loves everything pastel. She hates reality television but loves movies. She hates warm weather because she doesn't

like being hot. She hates being interrupted when she's speaking but loves interrupting me unintentionally and on purpose. She's sarcastic. She likes making jokes as long as she's not the butt of it. She hates when people baby her. She likes to plan things. She doesn't like change unless she needs to make a change, unless she's in control of what's changing.

She is all of these things, but she was still diagnosed two years ago when my parents found out she was skipping gym class for weeks during the gymnastics unit. She didn't want to take off her shoes to go inside the wrestling room. She didn't like the feeling of the mats.

For a while, all the kids saw her as the weird girl with a foot fetish and high functioning autism. When really, she's still the girl whispering fairytales underneath a pink polka dot bed sheet trapped inside a brain that works differently.

That's all it is.

It works differently.

That doesn't mean it doesn't work.

I still wake up some days and forget where I am. I have to sit up and remember I'm in a dorm room. Not the bed I grew up in. It's a second's worth of recollection, but something about it still stings. It weighs on my chest when I breathe, and I have to swallow before I speak.

The terrible feeling will fade in a few weeks. It always does.

But it hasn't faded for me yet.

"I miss you, too, Lay, I miss you, too."

CHAPTER FIVE: GOLDEN TICKET

"Let's go, puta!"

Stephanie quickly lowers the volume on her phone, but there's no use. We trade smiles because of her cousin's crude language. It's been the same routine the past three Friday nights. Stephanie gets the same "hurry up" message, a.k.a "Let's go, b*tch!" from Savannah before heading downstairs to meet up with her and Megan. Stephanie offered me an invitation to the dorm building basement shenanigans the first time around but didn't pressure me when I explained that I'm not into that kind of stuff.

I remain poised on my bed with my laptop on my lap, earbuds in my ears, and a random movie playing on the screen. It's eight o'clock, so I'm already in pajamas, including an oversized tie-dye shirt which is one of the many my sister and I spent two summers ago making. Really, I made them since Layla refused to touch the dye. She would also cringe because I paired the shirt with navy blue and green plaid pajama bottoms.

On the other hand, Stephanie still looks presentable even though she's sporting a messy low bun. She's wearing jeans, tan wedges, and a cream-colored knit tank top.

"Good?" She whirls around from her place in front of her desk and lightly pokes at the lip gloss she reapplied in

her small circle mirror. I give her a nod. She swipes up her wristlet.

"See you later." She chirps like she always does.

"Have fun!" I say back. "Stay safe." I always add because, as an older sibling, I can't help it.

"Thanks, mom!" Stephanie's tongue pokes out the door along with her head, but it's the smile she always ends the gesture with that lets me know she appreciates my concern.

Once the door clicks behind her, I click resume on my movie and snuggle further down against my pillows.

****

My ears are sore when I realize I no longer need my earbuds because I'm alone in the room. There are only ten minutes left in the movie, but I find myself too busy rubbing my ears to pay attention. I'm also too busy rubbing my ears to realize the buzzing and music are coming from my phone and not my laptop screen. I lift my laptop and my blankets. The cycle repeats a few times before my phone flies out of my sheets when I stretch them out over my head. I have a missed call from Stephanie by the time I pick my phone back up off the floor. I'm in the middle of typing her a text message when she calls again.

"Hello?"

"Hey, can you hear me?"

"Yes," I say, but refrain from pointing out I can also hear the beat of the song around her more.

"I'm sorry to bother you. Excuse me, excuse me, excuse me. Thank you." The music is muffled, and I hear the few clomps of Stephanie's footsteps before she sighs. "Sorry, can you still hear me?"

"Yeah, you okay?"

"Yeah, it's probably nothing, but I was supposed to meet up with this guy, but I haven't seen him yet. So, I started talking to this other guy, and he's not being pushy, but like—I don't know."

"Is Savannah with you?"

"She's too far gone, if you know what I mean, and the last time I saw her, Meg was taking her to the bathroom."

"Where are you?"

"I'm in the stairwell, and I would leave, but..."

"You still want to wait for the other guy?"

"Yes, but I also—it's probably nothing, but I only had one drink, and I already feel it. Like I know, you've never, but, like, I've done it enough to know I usually need more than one."

My stomach lurches as if I had the drink while my brain conjures up the worst.

"I don't know." Stephanie rushes out. "It could be nothing. This guy is just making me nervous. Like, he's not being forceful, yet he keeps looking at me. I don't know. What should I do?"

My stomach lurches again. "Um—" I try to put myself in her shoes, but that doesn't work because I know if I was in her shoes, I'd already be crying. So then, I pretend she's Layla, and it doesn't take long for my mama bear instincts to kick in. "I'll be there in five minutes."

"Are you sure? I'm sorry. It's probably nothing."

"It's fine. Which building are you in?"

"Kings."

"Give me, like, two minutes."

"Okay." She sounds a little distant.

I may be currently pulling my pajama pants off, one leg at a time and with one hand, but I still don't hang up.

"Lacie?"

"Yeah?" Now I sound a little strained, but it's only because I'm hopping on one foot because my sock decided to get stuck in the mix.

"Thank you." She breathes before ending the call.

I throw my grey sweatshirt on over my tie-dye shirt and a pair of dark jeans. My sneakers are thrown into the mix as well as my brown cross-body bag. I keep my hair in a high ponytail, but I pull my purple whistle out of my bag and slip it over my wrist. I close the door behind me as I tap on my cellphone flashlight.

I ditch the pathways and jog my way across the grass like the true mama bear I am, but I'm afraid the real sprint is going to be inside the building. Each dorm building is built three stories high and two rooms deep with the hallway in between. I can already hear the music as I trot down the stairs. I shouldn't be surprised when I push open the door. The basement parallels a football field. The only difference is this field is packed with people. The washing machines and dryers line the endzone at the opposite end of the room. Two long tables with chairs line the out of bounds, but they are covered with drinks and red solo cups. The rest of the room is cement.

I'm stuck on the outskirts. I'm at the opposite endzone with just a blank cement wall behind me. The room is crowded like the general admissions of a concert hall, but there are enough pockets to see the social networking. There's talking, dancing, and chugging, but not enough pockets to spot the pink and blue highlights I'm looking for. The pink and blue highlights that didn't stay on the stairs. She also doesn't seem to be by the makeshift DJ booth made out of two washing machines and light up speakers. The pop beat has already been embedded in my skull from here.

I take a step forward but step back when someone darts in my path. I get two steps into a pocket before getting shoulder bumped. At least the girl mumbles an apology. The guy who bumps into my other shoulder gives me that quick up and down look as he passes. Not in the "I'm-checking-you-out-how-you-doin'?" kind of way rather "who-what-when-where-and-why-the-f*ck-are-you-here?" kind of way.

I used to play the clarinet. I started when I was eight only because it was offered in school. I was forced to keep playing because it was either play the clarinet or sing in chorus. I chose to forge the six to eight hours of clarinet practice every week. When I was fifteen, I was ready to quit, but of course, there was this boy. He played the tuba. We would always lock eyes across the room above the music stands. He had braces and was the kind of boy who'd wear basketball shorts in the dead of winter. His arms fell down below his knees when he was sitting, and he'd always be the one making fart noises even when the tuba would bounce on his leg because he was nervous.

After months of nervous glances and ducking heads, with a few traded laugh smiles in between, I thought maybe—just maybe—there was something there. Maybe—just maybe—because we made enough eye contact every day like clockwork, maybe—just maybe—he thought I was cool, too.

I worked up the nerve to leave him a note on his locker with my name, my number, and a "hey, maybe let's hang out sometime." The same yellow post-it note he crushed inside his fist like a red solo cup as he checked the hallway for onlookers before tossing it in the trash.

The next time I walked into band class, I could feel the stares from all the other boys playing instruments in the

brass family. They snickered as they wiggled their trombone handles and blew into their trumpets while he hid his face behind the top of his tuba.

A few weeks later, he got his braces off and started dating the girl who sat in chair one playing the flute while I finally quit playing the clarinet. Even so, I've always felt stuck in chair three. Never good enough to be in chair one. Never someone's first choice. Never even picked at all.

I stand up on my tiptoes but fall back when the effort is futile. I'm an average height but throw in a couple of varsity sports players and high heels, and suddenly I'm a dollhouse amongst a bunch of skyscrapers.

I press Stephanie's contact in my phone before pressing my phone to my ear. I blame my worries for not trying this in the first place. It rings and rings. I press my right hand to my other ear, but she still doesn't pick up. Another bump to my shoulder, and my anger lashes out over my worry. All my emotions are thrown into my glare, but what I'm not expecting is a cartoon shark T-shirt and a double take.

"Peas!" The shout confirms my suspicions, but luckily the tall, lanky guy from the grocery store looks just as surprised. "Hey!" His eyes light up before he elbows the person behind him. The breath gets caught in the back of my throat when the guy's head turns. There's no hesitation or double take. His eyes zoom right in like a magnet. "It's peas!" Cute boy's friend throws his hands out in my direction, but it's unnecessary. Trent's already twisting his body around.

"Vanilla cake mix," he says.

"Lacie." I decide to rip the band-aid off all the food nicknames. "And, Trent, right?"

"Yes, and this is Zack." Trent flicks his hand out in

Zack's direction. Zack finally pulls his cup away from his lips and gulps down what he chugged.

"Zachary James Schmidt the Third, actually. Theater Major. Year Three." A beat passes before he shrugs and takes another swig from his cup. "I don't know. It felt right."

All three of us continue to stand in our little bubble. I'm fidgeting. Zack is bobbing his head to the music between flicking brown hair strands out of his eyes. Trent's standing way too still until he finally stuffs his hands in his front jean pockets and rocks back on his heels.

"So, I—" I start while Trent's lips part.

He rocks forward to ensure I can hear him over the music. "So, I think you're in my philosophy class?"

"On Mondays and Wednesdays?" I ask, even though my brain made the connection the second we locked eyes. That's a lie. My heart made the connection. It went *boom, splat* against my ribcage.

"Yeah, with Professor Collins."

Boom, splat. "Yeah."

Zack crushes his cup between his fingers.

"Lacie!"

I flinch when a hand clasps around my wrist, but I reciprocate the clasp when I see rose gold rings.

"I'm sorry." Stephanie's cheeks are flushed. "I didn't want to look suspicious. I figured I'd be better off in the crowd than by myself."

"It's fine." I clamp my other hand over hers. "Are you okay?"

"Yeah, let's get out of here." She goes to step forward and tug me along with her, but Zack steps into our path.

"*Wha-oh*! What's the rush?"

"Zack, Stephanie. Stephanie, Zack." I quickly motion

between them before Stephanie drags us around him.

"Attack," Zack says as he whips around. It would be an alarming phrase if he didn't lift the sides of his plaid shirt to reveal the cartoon shark is also paired with the hashtag: #ZACKATTACK. Stephanie bursts into laughter beside me while Zack tugs at Trent's T-shirt sleeve. He not only forces Trent to side-step into his shoulder but also awkwardly pivot his body around. "And you forgot Trent."

"Trent, Stephanie. Stephanie, Trent." I'm waving my hands around again, but it's as if I handed Trent the golden ticket to the *Willy Wonka Factory*. His smile stretches across his entire face, straining his cheekbones, and makes his head appear more like a circle than a square.

The music is still way too loud. I'm being shoved back into another random person's pocket while Stephanie begins tugging my arm in the other direction. Even as other people's heads and hair continue to dart across Trent's face, his gaze doesn't stray from mine, and his smile remains.

CHAPTER SIX: SIDEWALK CONVERSATIONS

It's not just Monday. It's another Monday. There's a difference. On the one hand, I should be happy about the difference because time is passing. On the other hand, I'd rather stay in bed all day than go to my classes.

"Is anyone sitting here?" A notebook gets tossed down on the table beside me before my eyes crawl up a grey sweatshirt covered Trent. "I don't want to be the guy that steals someone's seat a few weeks into the semester."

I usually sit alone. I'm used to sitting alone. When we were allowed to pick partners in class, I often opted to work by myself because it was easier than acknowledging that I had no one to choose. In the cafeteria, I would do homework while I ate my lunch because it helped distract me from the fact that the long rectangular table where I sat was usually empty.

His mouth tilts up to one side.

I shake my head. "No." I clear my throat. "You're good."

He unzips his sweatshirt with one hand and yanks the swivel seat out with the other. Luckily, there are more seats than people. Not only because people have stopped showing up regularly, but also this is the only hundred-person lecture hall in the building.

Trent opted for the seat one over from mine. His pen dangles from his mouth as he pushes himself slightly out from underneath the table. He's got the perfect laidback attitude for another Monday while I can never seem to sit without my legs crossed and completely tucked beneath me.

His eyes flicker up to meet mine, but mine flash back down to my phone in response. It's a terrible habit, along with the *boom, splat* that makes me forget whatever response I was going to type to Stephanie's text message.

****

Every class is ninety minutes. Lab classes are longer. But for sixty minutes of philosophy today, I'm able to pay attention and take notes like I have been the last few weeks. I'm able to pretend like it's just another Monday.

But it's no longer another Monday. It stopped being another Monday the second Trent decided to sit next to me and occasionally twirl his pen between his fingertips. Sometimes he'll even pass the pen back and forth between his hand and his mouth. Or even stretch his arms and his legs out.

That's all copacetic.

The problem is he's finally sitting still—for the most part. He's crouched over his notebook, and his legs are both tucked neatly under the table. While my hand is still trying to take down all the words coming out of Professor Collin's mouth, his pen is back to dangling from his lips.

Plato is hard to understand, let alone pay attention to. These past couple of weeks, I've been good at trying. The problem is Trent is now also hard to understand, let alone pay attention to.

I want to pay attention to Plato, not Trent, but Trent keeps turning his head in my direction. I can feel his eyes trail over the top of my head to the tip of my pen before he looks away.

He glances then looks away.

The pattern repeats enough times for me to catch on.

There are only a couple of minutes left in the lecture when he turns his head again, and I decide to turn mine.

He pulls his pen off his mouth, and his lips tip up to one side. The chalk squeaks, making me flinch and look away. My hand moves even faster against the page, and my letters are sprawling outside the thin blue paper lines because now Trent's shoulders are shaking. Even as he pushes his pen back into his lips, they are still cracked open to reveal his teeth.

Professor Collins drops his tiny chalk piece and gives me just enough time to glance at Trent again. This time in full, without reciprocation, I finally see he has his phone propped up behind his notebook. The phone I neglected to see from my periphery. This means he was never laughing at me, which should relieve me, and for the most part, it does. I can't remember the last time I took a full inhale since he sat down, and it doesn't seem like I will be any time soon. Not enough oxygen, only twenty-one percent, and *boom, splat*, I'm doomed.

****

"Finally." Trent breathes. I silently agree with him as I flip my notebook closed and push my chair back. It doesn't take long before I'm standing up and slinging my backpack over my shoulder. "Hey," Trent says before I can walk away. He slides his pen behind his ear as he stands. "How

do you do it?" He slings his backpack over his shoulder.

"Do what?"

He nods to the stage Professor Collins is still standing on as he maneuvers around the chairs. "Pay attention."

I don't know whether to smile or be confused. The crease between my eyebrows and the upward pull of my lip does a little bit of both as I shrug. "I don't know." I finally start trudging my way up the steps.

Trent falls into step beside me. "Are you a philosophy major?"

"No." I huff out a laugh while he catches the door from the person in front of us.

"Me either."

I wasn't necessarily expecting him to hold the door open for me, but since he does, I end up mumbling a "thank you" as I step out.

"So, what is your major?" Trent asks, falling into step beside me again.

"Biology," I say, "How about you?"

"Physical..." He shrugs his bag higher on his shoulder. "Education."

"Really?" I almost laugh. His eyebrows furrow as he holds the door open for me again, so I continue. "I just mean, you don't sound so sure."

"Oh." He smiles at the ground. "Yeah, I guess I'm not fully settled on it. It's really sports medicine, but my eventual goal is physical education, at least for now."

We continue to stand there on the pathway. Both of our sneakers are glued to the cement while other pairs of shoes scrape and scuff by us. I glance back up and find myself squinting to catch his eyes. He leans his head over and down a little to block the sun. Too bad the smile he flashes me with is almost as blinding.

"So, I guess I'll see you around."

I drop the hand I was using as a visor. "Yeah, I'll see you."

There he goes smiling again. There I go smiling back. There he goes walking backward. There I go watching him go. There's the early afternoon sun shining down on us, warming my skin when we both finally turn around. There goes the smile I consciously wipe off my face when I walk past other people but bounces back to life like the light off the grass.

CHAPTER SEVEN: PRESS

"What is that?" Trent's nose is all scrunched up, and I find myself shrinking down in my swivel chair.

It's now Wednesday, and my alarm didn't go off this morning, so instead of taking my daily jog across campus, I ended up taking a nice long sprint to class. I threw on my favorite grey sweatshirt. It's my favorite because it's baggy enough to cover my butt over leggings and curl my hands inside the sleeves if I want to feel like a cocoon, but it still hugs my body enough to feel like a cocoon as opposed to a sack. The problem is I don't remember the last time I washed it. I've been neglecting washing it because it still smells like the lavender-scented detergent my mom uses. After all these weeks, it still smells like home.

But it's pouring rain outside.

Today, I almost fell in the shower stall and took the practically see-through curtain with me. All so I could go outside and be showered again by mother nature and who knows what kind of smells.

"What?" I finally hiss when Trent leans over to sniff the air around me. My words falter on my notebook page as I find myself leaning away from him. He's still one seat away, but distance is futile if I know anything about body odor. Layla's lack of showers on the weekends are proof of that.

She'd live in her pajamas if she could.

Trent continues to bob his head around before leaning back into his own personal space. "Mm, you smell good. Like vanilla." He picks up his pen and slowly twirls it between his fingertips.

All the while, I sit back up and bring my sweatshirt sleeve to my lips. I guess it's better than smelling like—

****

"So, what else?" Trent asks the second Professor Collins finishes talking for the day. My hand is still trying to finish writing down the last bullet point, and I can feel my train of thought slipping away.

"What else what?" I ask, even though I'm more preoccupied with tugging my thought up before it slips into the canyon of oblivion.

"Vanilla cake, vanilla perfume." Trent's swinging his hand around in my peripheral vision.

I take a few more seconds to finish my scribbles before swinging my notebook closed. "That's it, though."

"Really?"

I shrug as I continue to pack up my things. Trent waits for me, but it's more like he has to since I'm blocking his way out of the row. I always feel like I'm rushing to pull myself together before and after my classes, but today it has more to do with the fact that he's standing there all leaned up against his pushed-in seat instead of the parade of people clomping up the stairs on my left. Even after I decide to stand up and ditch him, beelining for the door, he still tries to catch it and hold it open for me, forcing me to wrack my brain halfheartedly. It's harder now that all my thoughts seem to be falling over the edge.

"Vanilla tea?"

"Ah, I see." His eyebrows raise. "No coffee?"

"No coffee." I confirm.

"Me either. I prefer hot chocolate." He turns, walking backward the last few steps to the side exit of the Humanities building. He pushes the door open with his back but holds his black umbrella out in the entryway and slides it open before stepping outside. His lip is doing that upward tilt thing again as he glances back over at me. "Especially, the hot chocolate in the student center."

"I've never had it." I shrug as I tentatively step under the umbrella with him, but my shoulders jump a little when Trent gasps.

"Don't you live on campus?"

"Haven't you heard of Starbucks?" I forgot to mention, more specifically, vanilla chai.

Trent holds a hand over his heart. "I'm going to pretend you didn't say that."

I follow him a few steps further away from the building as the rain continues to pitter-patter against the top of his umbrella. People's feet also pitter-patter against the cement as some of them jog from building to building.

Trent shifts his backpack higher over his shoulder. "No, but seriously, you have to try it."

"Okay," I mock as I take a step back, but Trent closes the distance again.

"Wait, where are you headed next? I can walk you if you want?" He lifts the umbrella up in his hand as if to remind me he still has it.

"No, it's fine." I take another small step back, but he stretches his forearm out to keep the umbrella over my head. There's a chill in the air, yet he still only has a navy-blue T-shirt clinging to his chest.

"Are you sure?" He leans down, so I can hear him over all the raindrops. "It's not a big deal."

"Thank you, but—" My eyes keep darting to and from his. To and from his wispy blonde eyelashes. To and from the beauty mark above his eyebrow. To and from the acne scars coating his jaw. To and from all these things, I never imagined he'd have up close. I flick my thumb up over my shoulder. "I think I'm just going to run."

At least when I do, I have an excuse as to why my heart is beating so fast.

****

"Okay, that's it."

I barely pull my fingers away before Stephanie slams my laptop shut.

"Hey!" I whine, but she swipes it off my lap.

"Let's go."

"Where?" I ask.

"Somewhere." She groans as she slowly backs away from me and dramatically flops her back against her bed. Just her back because the beds are too tall to dramatically flop onto.

"I don't know," I say after I finish laughing at her antics.

"C'mon." She stands back up. "It's Friday night, and I don't feel like partying, but I want to do *something*." Now she's flopping her back against my bed.

"Food?" I offer.

She perks back up. "Movie?" A beat passes before Stephanie waves her hands from side to side. "Food and a movie?"

"Sure." I laugh.

Little did I know that "food" would mean stuffing

Stephanie's backpack purse with snacks from the vending machine downstairs. "And a movie" would mean an actual movie in the campus movie theater in the student center on a giant screen and not on the screens of our laptops.

We trek down the hill and across the quad, with Stephanie humming the whole way there.

"It's almost Halloween." She sing-songs. "Don't you love getting scared sh*tless!"

Layla would hate that Stephanie keeps messing around with her army green jacket zipper. Then again, she easily finds a new thing to dread every week, which is how you know she's doing okay. She went from missing me to complaining about being forced to journal in English class, to liking journaling but not wanting her teacher to read it, and now wanting journaling to be the only requirement instead of reading books, not by Nicolas Sparks.

"Will you stop," I say when Stephanie jokingly pulls up my black sweatshirt hood over my head for the hundredth time since we left the dorms.

"Never." She cackles like a witch. Next Friday, I'm pawning her off on Savannah and Megan.

"Oh, hey, peas."

I look up but silently curse for responding to the silly nickname while Stephanie is skipping ahead of me.

"Funny seeing you here." Zack spreads his arms over the long, round black desk in front of him. It takes up the whole right side of the entryway to the student center.

"How many jobs do you have?"

"Yup, I am broke, thank you for asking."

I throw him a sheepish smile. I thought I said that in my head. That's another thing I blame Layla for. Her lack of filter is contagious, a blessing and curse.

"So." He knocks his knuckles against the counter. "What

can I do for you?"

"Actually—"

"Is the theater booked up yet?" Stephanie's back at my side.

"It is Friday Fright Night," Zack says before turning slightly to click around on the computer. He's wearing a backward blue baseball cap, and there's a skeleton dog on the front of his shirt. "You're in luck. There are still some spots."

"Yes." Stephanie sounds way too excited, but I appreciate her energy. "Two tickets, please." We both slide over our IDs to pay the ten bucks while I see Trent walking in my periphery. It's like he's always there, always leaning and trotting and smiling. Even when he ducks his head after parting ways with who he was with and starts making his way in our direction. He's probably heading for the exit, but then he looks up, and, just like that, his grin is directed at me.

"Hey." Trent stops on the opposite side of Stephanie.

"Hey."

"I thought sharks lived in the ocean," Stephanie says.

Zack shrugs. "I'm more of a land shark."

Trent's eyes remain on me. "What's up?"

"I'm forcing Lacie to see her first scary movie," Stephanie answers for me.

"Not my first," I say before casting my gaze on my black high tops. "But definitely my last."

Zack seems to check an imaginary watch. "It looks like we've got ten minutes."

Stephanie cranes her neck back. "We?"

"Yup." Zack reaches under the desk, pulls out a triangular sign, and places it on top of the counter.

We're now Closed.
Student Help Desk Hours:
Mon-Fri 7 a.m. to 8 p.m.
Sat-Sun 7 a.m. to 6 p.m.

"Looks like you're stuck with me, *Steph-a-knee.*" Zack pretends to jump the counter before he laughs and decides against it. He goes around to exit from the other side.

"Ten minutes 'til what?" Trent asks.

Zack loops his arm around his shoulders once he's out on the other side. "We're going to see a scary movie."

"Yeah, no." Stephanie grabs my arm and starts gently tugging me forward.

Zack laughs. "I told you I don't bite."

I pass a glance back, which propels Trent to start moving again.

"So, you like scary movies?"

"Uh, not really."

I follow Stephanie to the right, down the basement stairs, and into the double doors that lead into the small theater resting beside a water fountain, a bathroom, and a janitor's closet.

"There's like no one here," Stephanie says, and she's right. Most of the red velvet seats are empty. There are a few couples and cliques, but it looks like most people had something better to do.

"See? Like I said." Zack passes us and walks ahead. "Stuck with me." There are only about thirty rows, from what I can tell, and he starts sliding into one towards the middle.

Stephanie struts forward and decides to slide into the row in front of him. He easily hops over into the seat on her right, leaving me to slide into the one on her left. Trent

takes the one beside me. It's only natural. At least, that's what I keep telling myself.

The lights are already dimmed, leaving us all cast in a light blue glow, but like Zack predicted, it doesn't take long for the movie to start to play. It must be on an endless loop from now until midnight. I run my fingers over the armrests and remind myself that whatever horrendous thing plays across the screen is not real. The problem is the red velvet also reminds me of the very real guy sitting next to me.

As usual, I'm distracted by Trent, but right now, I can't decide whether that's good or bad. Especially when he decides to slouch down against the back of his chair and let his feet slide with the motion. The outside of his left sneaker presses right up against the outside of mine. I don't dare look in his direction. His eyes are still trained on the screen in my periphery. That cancels out any intention. It has to. Plus, he's always slouching in philosophy.

A bang from the screen makes me jerk back in my seat, and although Stephanie chuckles at my reaction, I'm glad it forces Trent and I's feet apart.

I don't allow myself to be deceived by the sudden stillness on screen. It's the quiet before another storm. Or, in this case, more screams. I decided to focus on my surroundings again to prevent myself from getting sucked into eerie violin music and dark corners. The exit signs are still glowing red beside the large screen. I can see the wisps of hair on the tops of other people's heads. Stephanie's eyes are fixated on the screen, unlike a few minutes ago when they were cast on her phone. I slowly breathe in and run my finger along the chair cushion underneath me. For a second, I can pretend I'm calm.

Then I spot movement in the corner of my eye as

Trent's sneaker goes sliding again. Everything is still again when the outsides of our shoes are aligned. I fight the urge to assess his face, but I'm now more in tune with the movement beside me than anything on the screen.

He scratches his nose then the side of his cheek. A couple of minutes later, he runs his hands over the back of his neck but avoids deflating the spiked-up hair above his forehead. Then, he sits back up in his seat. Our feet disconnect by default.

I slowly lift my leg up and cross it over the other, separating us further because now I'm more irritated with myself for getting so worked up over nothing. I curl my hands into my sweatshirt sleeves and fold my arms across my chest as I sit up straighter. Then a ghost pops out the second I look ahead, making me flinch again.

This time Trent's the one quietly chuckling beside me, which makes my defensive posture futile. I'm not protected from the fictional horror nor the all too real boy beside me. Now would be a good time for Stephanie to yank my hood up. I'm about two seconds away from doing it myself.

"Hey."

I hear the whisper before Trent's posture is sliding again. Both his foot and thigh align with mine as he leans towards me this time.

"Are you okay?"

I catch his gaze for a split second before nodding. That's all I can do because even though I wasn't okay a second ago, his thigh is now providing my body more warmth than my sweatshirt—his jeans through my black yoga pants. I lift my head up to try and ignore it, but a hand comes up in front of my face.

"I wouldn't look yet."

A bang resounds, and for once, I'm the only one not flinching.

"Thank you," I whisper. He nods and drops his hand. The moment doesn't last long because more wails from the screen bring my own hands up to my face. I hesitate in planting them fully against my cheeks because my acne-prone skin doesn't need the contact, but also because I'm tempted to also cover my ears. I can't decide which is worse—the bloody scene or the screams.

I crack open my fingers. "Is it safe yet?"

"Nope," Trent whispers, then chuckles when I quickly cover my face again. Trent continues to look at the screen, but I keep my gaze on him. His skin continues to be filtered by whatever is running across the screen—white, blue, and black saturation. His side profile continues to go in and out of focus before he turns back to me.

"Now?" I whisper.

"Uh...yeah." He's scratching the back of his neck again.

"Don't lie."

He shakes his head. "I'm not, I swear."

"Okay." I slowly let my hands fall back down to my lap, but he leans forward.

"So." His fingers trace along the armrest. "How are you?"

"I've been better," I grumble both because it's true and because I still don't want to disrupt any other moviegoers even though, at this point, I probably already have. Then again, Trent keeps chuckling as if we're watching comedy.

I go to pick at the blue paint on my nails, but my eyes dart up again on their own accord. Natural instincts I want to curse but can't because a piece of hair falls over my face, and Trent's pointer finger comes up from the armrest and gently pushes it to the side. The action is so minimal I

barely feel it.

"You know," Trent whispers. "I could have saved you."

"From what?"

"From"—he pauses as someone screeches on the screen— "this."

"How?"

"If I had your number."

My lips press together. "Smooth."

His lips part for a second, but he quickly clamps them shut. "But, I—it's true."

"Sure."

"Because you could have texted me."

"Okay."

"And I would have said…" I go to look at the screen, but he throws his hand up again. "I would have asked if you wanted to go get some hot chocolate, or ''

Another scream.

"Some tea."

I hear another squeal, but this time it's from the little cartoon version of me that runs around in my head. For some reason, I picture her in the sweaty gym shorts and high ponytail back in aisle three as she pops confetti.

"Yeah, okay." I clear my throat, but my body still feels like it's buzzing.

Trent keeps his hand up, leaving me only to hear the choking coming from the screen. Even Stephanie seems to cower a little in her seat. Zack has been slouched since he sat down. He may even be sleeping with the shift in his baseball cap.

"Hey, Lacie?"

"Yeah?"

Trent looks sheepish when I finally turn my head. "Can I have your number?"

I raise my eyebrow on the outside, but on the inside, the little cartoon version of me blinks and blinks her heart eyes before melting into a colorful puddle. Now I know what it feels like to be one of the girls on the screen. The girl everyone makes fun of because she walks toward the danger rather than running far, far away from it.

I pull my phone out from my bag and hand it over to Trent, who, I don't realize until later, adds himself as *Red Velvet*.

CHAPTER EIGHT: HOT CHOCOLATE CONVERSATIONS

Since Trent and I exchanged numbers, the conversations often started with questions about philosophy readings and funny pictures. At some point, though, he texted me about trying the hot chocolate again. Damn him and that hot chocolate, but not really. I don't mind him or the hot chocolate. I do mind that he and hot chocolate put together are making me sweat. I don't want to sweat. I shouldn't be sweating because it's just Trent and hot chocolate. I shouldn't have said yes. Really, all I said was "sure," but I shouldn't have because then I wouldn't be sweating so much, and my heart wouldn't be counting each step closer to the student center.

When you walk into the student center, Starbucks is in the back-right corner. It has its little nook with a window divider wall separating the order line and the crowd waiting to pick up. It's lined with crisscrossing orange wood that matches the three small wooden tables and one-sided bar. Even though I prefer tea, the smell of warm coffee and caramel that wafts through the air is always tempting. The line can get long, especially during the lunch rush between morning and afternoon classes, but if I opt to go to the

student center during the day, I'm more often swerving to the right.

Today, I swerve left. It feels funny. It feels like my legs want to go one way, muscle memory, the right way, but the rest of my body leans in towards the left, and my feet scramble to catch up.

I willingly head into the maze, a.k.a. the food court slash student lounge. The allure of the comfortable coffee bean smell is traded for lunch meat and waxy floor cleaner. All the food options and lines outline the perimeter of the room, while there are rectangular and circular tables scattered about the center. None of which are filled to the brim at this time of day, but most are occupied. The usual hustle and bustle of lunchtime has quieted down and given way to late afternoon whispers. I inhale and exhale and look around as if I've been here a thousand times, but social Darwinism kicks into high gear. Every gaze that reciprocates mine feels like laser eyes that see through my façade. The lions, the tigers, the bears—oh my—they know I never come in here. I'm a fish out of water. They have to know, but really, they don't know. They don't care. They could probably care less. It only takes a split second for them to look up and look back down. Sometimes it feels like survival of the fittest. One look snaps your confidence like a twig when really everyone's mind is swirling with to-do lists and funny memes.

It doesn't help that the second I left my dorm, my heart crashed in at full speed ahead—no seatbelt or airbag. Just pure collision against my ribcage again and again and again. I'm almost mad when I spot Trent because it's all too easy. It's all too much. Him and his long-sleeve t-shirt. Him and his perfectly gelled hair.

I slowly maneuver my way around people's chairs. I may be walking at a normal pace, but on the inside, it's all in slow-motion—every bend of the muscles in my foot. Each inhale and exhale through my chest. Each curl of my fingers as they tighten around my cross-body bag.

He's sitting on the end of one of the rectangular tables. The closer I get, the more I notice that his jean cover leg is bouncing up and down to the same erratic beat inside my chest.

"Hi," I say the second my stomach hits the edge of the table.

"Hey." He looks up, and everything is still, but the slow-motion wears off the second my butt hits the bottom of the plastic chair. There are two brown paper cups sitting between us. They have yet to have their plastic lids cracked.

I glance back up, and another twig snaps. It might even be my rib from one final pound against my chest because Trent is just a blob of color in my periphery. Here he is up close and completely saturated. No overcast sky or umbrella or movie theater darkness to filter him. Every time we lock eyes, it feels like the first time in aisle three.

"Are you ready?" One simple question, one simple tip of his lips, and there he is—the fidgeting guy from philosophy. He rubs his hands together like a master magician. "So, the only issue I have is it's usually too hot to drink right away, so…" He pops the lid off the cup closest to him before reaching over and doing the same to mine. "We have to wait."

Steam flutters out of the dark brown liquid, and I cup my hands around the cup. All I can think about is convection. Warm air rises, cool air falls.

"This is my favorite part about hot drinks," I say. "It's

like my own little bubble of warmth."

Trent's fingers circle his cup. "Is that your favorite part about biology?" He wiggles his eyebrows. "Heat transfer."

I fight the urge to roll my eyes. "I think that's chemistry."

"But I thought the sun—"

"More earth science." I scrunch my nose before we lock eyes. He seems torn between his amusement and the train of thought I just put to a screeching halt. This is far from a competition, but I'll take the lull in the dialogue—I'll take the win.

"So." His lips finally part again. "What do you like about biology then?"

"That," I say.

This time his eyebrows furrow. "What?"

My lips quiver. "The conversation we just had."

"You like making people confused?"

"No." I laugh. "I like that it's an umbrella, or no, more like the soil—yeah, the soil that all the other sciences essentially grow out of."

His amusement returns. "I thought that was earth science."

"Yeah, but we wouldn't be studying the earth if we didn't exist. There would be no chemical reactions and transfers if things weren't living and acting and changing and growing. Physics is only the way things act biology is—" I stop mid-sentence because Trent's eyes remain over my shoulder.

He flicks his hand out in a quick wave but ends up sitting up straighter and providing the person with a more energetic one.

"Sorry," he says when he slumps back down. "Please

continue." He waves his hand in a circle before wrapping his fingers around his jaw.

"No, it's okay. I was kind of rambling anyway."

"No, you were making sense." His lips tilt upward, but he hides the expression behind his hand as he rubs the light stubble on his jaw. "But you were starting to sound a little Professor Collins-esqe."

I sink down against the back of my seat. "Sorry."

"Don't apologize. It's your major. It would be weird if you weren't passionate about it."

We trade smiles before I wave my hand. "Well, what about you? Why did you choose physical education or sports medicine or whatever?"

"I guess I sort of fell into it." He shrugs. "Since I sometimes like to volunteer at the school where my mom works for their summer camp. It's like an outdoor gym class every day."

"That sounds fun."

"It is." He smiles. "I mean, sometimes it's way too hot, but I like playing with the kids. I like seeing the kids outside and interacting with each other." He chuckles a little. "You know before and after the cootie-phase." My nose scrunches up a little, making him continue. "You know the time before and after girls have cooties. At first, everyone can be superheroes, and then eventually, we get "no girls allowed" and cliques and wolf packs. You know, biology."

"Wolf packs?"

He waves his hand. "You know what I mean."

I find myself sitting up a little straighter on a laugh. "I hate to break it to you again, but that's also not biology."

"But you know, it's like a natural thing, I guess, as we get older."

"I don't know about that." I laugh again. "As far as I know, boys are the ones that still have the cooties—and the wolf packs."

Trent leans forward. "Am I not allowed to talk about girls and bathrooms?"

"No, you may not."

He holds his hands up. "I'm just saying."

"And I'm just saying…" I raise my brows as I lean back in my chair. "Boys and locker rooms."

"Girls and brunch?"

"Brunch?" I laugh. "Boys and gyms."

"Girls and the mall."

"Harsh stereotype. Target is where it's at, but boys and sneakers."

His mouth opens and closes. "Sneakers aren't a place."

"Still a cult."

"Wolf pack."

"Wolf pack. Whatever." My head rolls back as if I'm annoyed, but my lips continue to quiver, showing otherwise.

Trent seems to be having a similar problem, also fighting off his smile. We level our gazes for a beat. The amusement only makes his eyes burn brighter. It's easy to forget where we are, the fact that we are still surrounded by a dozen other people. Once again, it's not a competition, but it sort of feels like it right now. After weeks of communicating through mumbles and notebook paper scraps, this feels like testing the water, filling bottles, and shaking them up to ensure the pH is balanced. If it's too red it means too acidic, which equals clashing and wearing out. Too blue though, means too basic and not enough to keep us coming back.

It takes low laughter and the scraping of some chairs for our contest to be over.

Trent halfheartedly puts his hand up again. "Point taken." He combs his fingers through the front of his hair a few times. It immediately springs back up each time, but I blame the gel and comb he must use instead of any natural tendencies. "But that's all I really want." He continues after dropping his hand back down to his lap. "To promote kids staying active and having fun. And if I don't become a gym teacher, I would love to open a recreational camp like that or help kids in some way."

"Sounds cool." I'm nod. "At least—"

Trent stretches back. His shoulder blades pull together behind him before he freezes. "Hi!" He laughs at more people over my shoulder. "I see you, Josh. You too, Asher." He sends them a wave.

It'd be more awkward if I turned around, so I don't, but I can't decide if all these commercial breaks seem too calculated or too comical to be real.

"Sorry," he mumbles again, slumping back down in his seat, repeating the same jaw rubbing and smiling behind his hand process. "What were you saying?" He offers from behind his hand and pulls me back into reality: my numb butt and all.

"Oh, nothing." I cross and uncross my legs. "At least you have a plan. You could probably even do both, you know? Gym teacher and recreational center."

Trent waves his hand. "We'll see, but you also sounded like you knew what you were going to do."

I huff out a laugh through my nose. "I don't know. I mean, sure, I want to do something in my field, but I don't know what I want to do."

"That's okay," Trent's voice softens, but I can only bring myself to shrug. "No, seriously, it's okay not to know. You think Zack knows what he's doing half the time?"

I laugh even though I doubt it's entirely true. I pass a glance at the time on my phone from inside my bag. I have my late lab today, but we still have time. The student lounge has only gotten louder, though, making me lean forward in my seat.

"I guess it's just—" I hesitate, but Trent's eyes don't stray from mine, so I continue. "I guess what bothers me is that we are expected to know. Like, the second someone finds out your major, they automatically ask, 'So, what are you going to do with *that*?'"

"That's true." Trent chuckles, but my train of thought continues to spill out into the open.

"It just bothers me that they say we don't have to have it all figured out, yet they expect us to have it all figured out. How they say it's not all about money, yet they also want us to show them the money."

"Yes." Trent breathes out another laugh as he nods. "And that's why Professor Collins said the world is all a bunch of bullsh*t."

The mention of the tangent from one of the philosophy lectures turns on a light bulb in my head. "But I think that's why Socrates and all the other philosophers kept calling bullsh*t in ancient society too."

Trent holds up his pointer finger as his lips part, but my eyes dart up on their own accord.

"Hi, Trent." A group of four or five girls coo at the same time. Some of their eyes flicker down to me as they pass around his shoulder to get to the line forming a few

tables away. There's no social Darwinism in their gazes. No jealousy or snarl. Rather genuine curiosity, like the casual observers of a brand-new species, fascinated and enamored with every movement, and yet it still makes me squirm just the same.

Trent lifts his hand up in a wave before folding it back over his chest while they seamlessly go back to their conversations, forgetting my very existence.

"Sorry." He doesn't hide his unease this time as he scratches at his elbow before reaching for his jaw again. "I blame Zack." He pushes his fingers into his skin and pulls it forward. "He dragged me into a bunch of clubs our freshman year."

I laugh. "He must know what he's doing then."

"Yeah, bothering me." Trent runs a hand through his hair. This face-to-face thing has me thinking he's more like a puppet. His actions are almost always too perfect—too calculated. His eyebrows, his lips, his hands are all always being pulled up and down. Forward and back. He leans forward again as if to prove my point.

"He's your best friend?" I say as more of a question than a statement.

"My worst friend." He feigns a groan before pausing as his eyes glue to the table. A memory seems to flash behind his eyes that makes him smile. "Nah, he's cool."

"Cooler than you?"

"Hell no." He shakes his head as he wraps a hand around his cup again. "Okay, fine. A little."

"That's what I thought." I laugh and pass a glance at my phone again, but too quickly to really absorb the time.

Trent rubs his hands together again before I catch on to more eyebrow wiggling. "Ready?" he asks when our eyes

lock.

"Ready."

We gently tap our cups together in cheers before I bring mine to my lips.

He raises an eyebrow. "So?"

"It's good," I say after I swallow. "But I think we waited too long."

He grimaces a little as he takes another sip. "True."

"I guess we talk too much." I tease, but he tips his cups in my direction as his lips lift to one side.

"Who said that was a bad thing?"

CHAPTER NINE: MIDTERMS AND NIGHTMARES

"*Ugh*." Savannah groans before slurping up the last of her black iced coffee. "Midterms can officially suck my ꞏꞏꞏ"

"Savannah!" Stephanie yells and shoves her shoulder before she can finish her sentence.

Savannah doesn't even reciprocate the shove. Instead, she slams her laptop closed and hops off Stephanie's bed. "Dios mío. I'm f*cking hungry."

"More like f*cking crazy," Stephanie grumbles back.

I blink my eyes a few times before giving in and rubbing them. All the words sprawled out across my laptop screen look small, and when I pass a glance at the notebook on my lap, it resembles alphabet soup more than any coherent information. The only midterm I've survived so far is for my lab class, and the weight that lifted from my workload was relieving but minimal. I reluctantly bring my hands back up to my keyboard and attempt to keep typing up my review sheet for my philosophy midterm tomorrow. It's an in-class writing assignment, and he gave us six possible prompts. You would think that would narrow things down, and to an extent, it does. For my black and white, hypothesis and conclusion, this is this, and here is the

proof kind of brain—the possibilities when it comes to analyzing philosophical literature make my head spin a little more than usual.

It doesn't help that Trent made it his goal to blow the biggest bubble gum bubble with the most silent pop during the review last class. He failed miserably—so miserably— that I only had a second to choke down a laugh as the whole lecture hall went silent, and everyone's swivel chair swiveled in our direction.

"Sorry." Trent lifted his hand in an apology to Professor Collins.

"You should be," he bellowed back before continuing to lecture.

"*Ugh.*" Megan sighs, not as disgusted as Savannah's groan but just as tired. "I'm done, too."
I see Savannah push Stephanie's desk chair in my periphery, sending Megan for a spin around. Stephanie traded her original wooden desk chair last weekend for a big black one. It takes up a few more inches of already dwindling space and squeaks a little every time before it reaches a full three-sixty.

However, Savannah decides to keep pushing, making Megan squeal a little bit. I glance over my shoulder as Megan grabs her phone and begins filming herself. I wonder how she's not dizzy before Savannah pushes against the back of the chair too hard, and it almost goes crashing to the ground. Almost since Megan throws her hand out to grip Stephanie's desk, while Savannah lunches forward and grips the arms.

"All right, fools." Stephanie hops down from her bed. "Let's go get some food." There's some rustling as they all pack up their things before my notebook gets yanked from my lap. "You're coming, too."

"But." I start to protest as Stephanie tosses my notebook on my bed.

"No, buts, we've been studying for, like, two hours."

I throw her some half-joking disbelief, and she laughs as she slaps my arm.

"Fine, maybe only *you've* been studying for two hours, but whatever. You still need food." She kicks the back of my chair with the toe of her shoe, making me realize how numb both my butt and legs are.

"Fine." I give in as I stand and stretch my arms up. "But we'll still study after, right?" I send my eyes around to each of them as I throw my black windbreaker on over my long-sleeve shirt.

"Right." They all respond in unison, but they all drag out the word like lying little kids and drag me out of the room before I can say anything else.

****

I suck in a deep breath as I remember where I am. My muscles are tense and weighted as I try to roll over with heavy eyelids. My heart is thundering in my chest, moving its way up in my throat. I try to even my breathing, but I see black hoodies and a van as soon as my eyes close again. They still have their hands on my arms and my legs and around my neck.

I force my eyelids open, blinking and blinking as I roll on my back and will myself to breathe. My lungs feel like they shrunk down two sizes, while my heart grew times three, beating and beating me from the inside out.

I push back my comforter and reach for my phone charging on the window ledge. It's only four thirty-four in the morning. I sit up. All the ordinary things in daylight are

shadowy configurations at night. While my mind lulls to go back to sleep, I can't shake the cold sweat.

I get up and pick up the lid of my trunk and dig around, feeling at my clothes for the scratchy waterproof fabric of my athletic shorts. I replace my polka-dotted pajama bottoms with them, keep my oversized t-shirt on, and grab the nearest sweatshirt I can find. It almost still feels like I'm dreaming as I stuff my feet into my sneakers and grab my phone, especially once I'm blinking against the flickering yellow hallway lights and start jogging out of the building.

I throw open the dorm building door, and it clatters back against the bricks. The frigid morning air feels like a fresh slap in the face, but I greedily breathe it in. It should be enough to pull me out of the haze, but I still feel a shake in my knees that propels me forward onto the cement pathway. My sneakers scrape and pound along, finally coming in sync with the pounding inside my chest. I don't know where I'm going, but as long as I keep moving, it is easier to forget.

The sky starts as a dark blue. The colder weather always postpones the sunrise, but it soon starts fading into lighter shades. The frosty haze coating the buildings starts to peel away, leaving behind the dewy grass and tree bark.

An hour passes before I walk back towards the dorm buildings. I gulp in all the oxygen I momentarily forgot I needed as the adrenaline fades and leaves just endorphins in its wake.

"I don't know how you do it." My mom used to joke when I'd come home drenched in buckets of sweat.

"It's the morphine." I'd jokingly stick my tongue out.

My heart pings a little at the thought of my mom. Bad dreams can follow you anywhere, but sometimes this whole campus still feels like a bad dream. Especially on the

really bad days, when I'm texting Layla and yearning for my lilac room and movie nights snuggled up on the couch.

I step around some geese poop before noticing something red walking the opposite way across the grass. It feels like a movie. Out of all the people on campus, the night and shining armor in a bright red windbreaker jacket is trudging through the misty early morning haze. Only his wet sneakers sink into the ground a little bit, making his slow-motion walk more like begrudging clomps. He also seems to be wrestling with the silver spiral binding of his notebook that looks caught in his zipper.

Trent looks up and freezes. The perfect action shot. If only his face didn't scrunch up. "Lacie?"

"Trent?"

He lifts a hand up and cups it around his mouth. "Lacie-e e." He mocks an echo.

My lips curl up, but I still send him a now redundant wave before he starts clomping his way over to me.

He waves his arm like a showman. "What light through yonder window breaks?" He pauses and stands straight again. "And that's all I got."

I laugh. "Zack would be very disappointed."

"I know. You know he's played Romeo four times, actually?"

"Really?"

"Yeah, fifth-grade talent show, seventh-grade drama club, and then two back-to-back summer Shakespeare festivals the year before and after we graduated high school."

"Wow." I glance back up at the sky. It's more of a periwinkle blue, like the flowers on my comforter, reminding me of sleep and the day I'm now dreading to start. "I envy his memorization skills."

"Me too," Trent says around the pen he has back in his mouth. He wrestles with his notebook and zipper again. "Finally!" he sighs, catching his pen with one hand and straightening his jacket with the other. "That's why I'm up." He lifts his notebook as he looks back up. "Cramming."

"At five a.m.?"

"Yeah, I get too distracted in my room sometimes, and I have a book reflection paper for Sport and Exercise Psychology that I procrastinated about. I've got—" He reaches inside his jacket pocket to check his phone. "Exactly nineteen hours and counting."

"But five a.m.?"

He smiles a little, and I remember I must look like the old hag in Snow White, only my bedhead isn't hidden under a cloak, rather swinging high in a ponytail. I also probably have the morning breath to match the yellow teeth.

"Zack's snoring certainly doesn't help."

I nod as I go to turn. "Gotcha. I'll let you get to it then."

"No, wait." He clears his throat. "What are you doing up?"

"Just running." I shrug.

His eyebrows raise. "At five a.m.?"

"Ha, ha, I get it." I run a hand over my head and through my ponytail. "I just…couldn't sleep."

"Ah, story of my life. Are you on your way back then? I'll walk you."

"No, it's okay. I don't want to distract you."

"Nah, you can help me. I'll run my paper idea by you."

I chuckle. "I don't know if I can be much help, but okay."

We start walking down the pathway for a few minutes.

The wind blows around and billows Trent's jacket. I switch my hair into a low ponytail, all the while knowing my eyes are still glassy. I blink and blink, but most of what Trent's talking about seems to go right over my head, and it's not because I don't understand what he's saying, but rather my brain won't shut up. Everything I have to do today, class, reading, prepare for lab later, what will I eat, will I get a chance to catch up on some sleep, continues to circle my head on a continuous loop.

I pass a glance to the left. Trent stares back at me, so I quickly look down, but I still feel his gaze burning into the side of my head.

"Sorry, I must be boring you to death."

"No, not at all." I don't sound convincing. "I'm sorry, I'm tired."

"So, you decided to go on a run?"

"Well, when you put it like that." My gaze finds the place where the buildings meet the sky. "I needed a distraction."

"Ah, I see. Running away from your midterms?"

"Yeah." I huff out a laugh. "Basically."

We walk a few more steps in silence. Our feet scrape against the cement as some landscapers start pouring out from behind the buildings, passing each other greetings and pointing and nodding at things.

"Do you run every morning?"

"Yeah, I try. At least during the week."

"At five a.m.?"

I crack a smile. "Not usually."

Another beat passes as the dorm buildings come into view.

Trent's steps are slow. "Which one?"

"Oh, Pemberley."

Trent nods and follows me as I cut across a large patch of grass. He flicks a thumb over his shoulder. "I'm over at Kings."

"Ah." I send him a look as I dig my hands into the front pocket of my sweatshirt. "The party palace."

He chuckles. "That's the one."

We step back onto the pathway, and I almost regret cutting through. I have a chilling ring of water surrounding my toes.

Trent stops walking. "Hey, Lacie?"

"Yeah?" I glance back, only a step ahead.

He takes a step. "I'm not trying to pry or anything, but…are you really okay?"

I laugh. "I know I look a little crazy."

"No, that's not it. I mean—" He passes a glance at my feet. "You are wearing fuzzy socks."

"It was still dark, okay?"

He holds his hands up. "I'm not judging. Just checking."

"I'm fine now, really." I run another hand over my hair. "It's silly." I wave my hand.

"No." Trent's voice is soft as he takes another step forward. "Tell me."

"It's silly." I huff out another laugh, but I sober up when his gaze doesn't stray from my feet. I fidget a little in response. "I had a bad dream, that's all." Trent looks up, so I continue. "And I've always had bad dreams. I mean, it's not that bad anymore, but at one point when I was little, it got bad. It always involved me being kidnapped, or— worse." I gulp. "I guess because, since I'm a woman, I've always been on high alert, and the weird thing is, when I was little, I couldn't control the dreams, and that's why I would get so scared. Now, especially in the last few years,

I'm sometimes able to control it, in the sense that I can be conscious enough to know that I'm dreaming, which makes me better at trying to outsmart them. I'm able to do all the things, like call 9-1-1 or hide in a certain place, or trick them into thinking I'm going one way, but then going another, but the scary part is, no matter how many times I get away, they still end up catching me in the end."

Another breeze rolls by, reminding me of our surroundings. The hooded figures in my imagination aren't lurking in the shadows, but sometimes they still feel like they're breathing down my neck.

"That is scary," Trent finally says.

I take a step back. "Yeah, but still silly."

"No, it's not." He mimics my step. "I've never thought   I mean, we all have had dreams sometimes, but I   I never thought as a girl, I mean, women, you know, female." He clears his throat, making my lips quiver a little. He notices, and his lips seem to do the same before he shakes his head. "All I'm trying to say is I guess I take it for granted sometimes. My fears, although valid, will never compare to yours in that sense."

My eyebrows furrow a little. "I guess I never really thought of that either."

Another pause passes between us before it feels right to start walking again. The back of Trent's hand grazes mine as we fall back into step.

"I'm guessing that's also why you don't like scary movies."

I purse my lips at the urge to smile again. "Pretty much."

"You know when I have a bad dream." His smile is as lopsided as his head. "I picture Zack in a coconut bra and hula skirt."

I stop in my tracks. My eyebrows draw together as my

mind conjures up the image of a cartoon t-shirt covered Zack with a coconut bra on top, and I'm sputtering before I can help it. "No way!"

Trent lets out a few chuckles himself. "Okay, maybe not. But I've seen it."

I look back up. "No!"

"Yes! Our eighth-grade graduation dance was Hawaiian-themed, and he decided to take it to the next level." He raises his hand as if raising an imaginary bar. "Hula skirt and all."

"No way." I laugh again.

"Let's just say the teachers weren't pleased."

"I can imagine." I'm still smiling as we start walking again.

We finally make it to my dorm building, and I find my eyes flickering between the door and Trent.

"Thank you for walking me."

"No problem." He nods.

"And for listening."

A smile traces his lips as he goes to rub at his eyes. "No problem." He alternates between rubbing and blinking for a second before meeting my gaze again. "I would say the same but…"

"Crap! I'm sorry, do you want to tell me now?"

"No, don't worry about it." He's still smiling as he tugs his notebook further into his side. "I'm not worried about it."

I take a step back. "Well, if you hit any roadblocks while writing, you can text me."

"Sounds good."

Another beat passes as we both linger on opposite edges of the pathway. The rising sun in the sky is casting an orange halo around the tops of the buildings.

"I'll see you later then." I offer as my body leans in towards the building, but my feet still don't move.

"Yeah." Trent stuffs his other hand into his pocket. "And you know…"

I tear my eyes away from my fuzzy, striped socks.

"You know you can always call me if you want." He shifts his stance as his heel hits the grass. "I'm a light sleeper."

"Thank you."

We lock eyes as he takes another step back.

He bows forward. "Sleep dwell upon thine eyes!" He straightens back up and pauses. "Okay, so I lied. But who do you think read lines with him?" He laughs and lifts the hand he has stuffed in his pocket, sending me a final penguin flap kind of wave before turning around.

I watch as the red of his jacket swishes from side to side as the toe of his sneaker squishes into the grass with a lighter step than when I first saw him earlier. It's the same lightness that swells inside my chest as I'm shot with another round of endorphins that, for once, I didn't have to pound into my system. They float into my bloodstream like dandelion seeds in the wind.

I turn and push down on the door handle only to realize I forgot my ID. Time of death, six-seventeen am, because Stephanie's going to kill me.

CHAPTER TEN: BOOZY RED VELVET

The pink and blue highlights in Stephanie's dark hair make a pattern down her back. It took her less than ten minutes to pull all the curls back and fishtail braid them. She's using her hand as a visor as she surveys the crowd in front of us, but unlike me, she doesn't have to stand on her tiptoes.

"*Ugh*." She groans as she whirls back around to face me. That's how I know she isn't looking for Savannah or Megan, but rather the guy she was supposed to meet up with. "He said he was going to text me, but the service down here sucks." She glances down at her phone while I attempt to glue myself to the cement wall beside us as people continue to spill out of doors a few feet behind us.

Sneakers squeak and scuff against the floor while the music swallows the clicking of people's heels. I do take note of some cute boots. Some have buckles, some have heels, and some have buckles and heels. Stephanie was going to wear her tan booties but opted for sneakers last minute when she saw I was wearing mine.

"Hey, look who it is!" Zack's head pops up behind Stephanie's shoulder, backward baseball cap, plaid shirt, and all. "Peas and Steph-a-knees."

"Far-left table," Stephanie mumbles as she glances up from her phone. Her gaze completely bypasses Zack as she stands up on her tiptoes. She emits a little squeal as she

waves before she turns back around and gives my wrist a quick squeeze. "Wish me luck!"

"Good luck." I smile. "Be careful!" I yell over the music for good measure.

"Whoa, hold up." Zack reminds me of his presence. I also finally catch on to the wisps of Trent's hair behind his back. "Peas can't stand alone. They come in a pod."

I laugh and even go as far as to shove his arm a little because the joke and nickname are getting old, but then I pull my hands back and tap my fingertips against the wall. "I'm Stephanie's wing-women tonight."

"Whoa, wait a minute." Zack's head rears back this time. His eyes ping-pong between the crowd of people in front of us and me a few times before he yanks Trent in front of him. "Not on my watch." I only hear Zack's words because he shoves Trent into me.

"Zack!" I yell as my hands shove into Trent's chest to keep it from colliding with my face.

Trent's sneaker-covered feet only continue to stumble forward, and I grab a fistful of his navy-blue thermal with one hand and grip his bicep with my other to keep him from falling on top of me. What makes it worse is I can feel the vibrations of his chuckles through the waffle-patterned cotton material of his shirt. It's those uncontrollable chuckles paired with his haphazard attempt at shuffling his feet that make me realize there must be more than blood running through his veins. The thought forces me to finally maneuver Trent, so he's propped up against the wall beside us. I finally let go when I know he's not going to collapse.

"Vanilla!" His eyes are all glassy and unfocused, and his cheeks are flushed.

"Hi," I say but find myself leaning closer only because

a new song begins to play, and it's filled with more heavy words as opposed to a heavy beat. "Are you okay?"

"I—" He starts but pauses to push his right hand into the wall and nudge his shoulder a little further up. "I am wonderful." He throws his hand out as if to prove it, but his shoulder ends up slipping again. "How are you?" Trent coos out the "you" as he slides himself not only up but closer to me.

I pass a glance to my right and catch on to some cheering from one of the tables, but all I can see are people's backs, arms, shoulders, and necks. Too many people. Too many backs. Too many arms. Too many shoulders. Too many necks. All this alcohol and sweat.

I reach into my tan crossbody bag to try and catch the time on my phone but glance back up because Trent's gaze is unwavering. His lips are tilted up, which is nothing new, but his freshly shaven cheeks are sheen with sweat. He has another beauty mark on the side of his nose, right between his nose and his eye, which matches the small, round brown one above his right eyebrow. Under different circumstances, I maybe would've questioned why it's another thing I haven't noticed before, but he's still teetering on the wall like a broken tree branch.

I reach into my bag again and send Stephanie a text.

Trent's drunk. Going to help him to his room.

I make sure it sends before zipping my bag back up and turning around to face him entirely. He attempts to mimic my motion but ends up leaning the side of his head against the wall instead of his hands.

"C'mon," I say more to myself than to him as I gently grip onto his arms and attempt to pull him forward. He not only gives me no resistance but also no help as I manage to guide him to the double doors leading upstairs.

We almost get trampled by some people coming down the first set of stairs, but I pause to wrap his left arm around my shoulders once we make it to the first landing.

"Where's your dorm?"

"My room." He hums.

"Yes, your room." I almost laugh.

"You're taking me to my room."

I see the slightest flash of his teeth, and I fight the urge to roll my eyes by tugging him forward. "Yes, but it's not like that. What floor is it?"

"Second." He hums again, while I can't seem to catch my breath as I continue to drag him alongside me up the stairs.

"You're heavier than you look," I grumble when we make it to the first-floor landing.

Trent is still humming. He even flops his right arm onto his head and allows his elbow to drag against the wall as I pull him up the last flight of stairs to the second floor. I drop his arm from around my shoulders and go back to tugging once we make it to the beginning of the hallway.

"Do you have your ID?" I walk backward in front of him but have to slow down when I realize he's stumbling.

"I'm close enough, okay? Just a couple more months."

I stop in my tracks. "For your room, Trent."

"*Oh*." He drags out the word long enough for the girls passing by to throw us a look. He uses his open hand to feel the back of his jeans, but when he only continues to pat his backside, I let go of his other hand. He holds his ID up for me to see before latching on to my arm again. "Follow me." He not only drags out the "me" but also manages to drag me forward a few more steps before stopping in front of a door. His face scrunches up as he stares at the tan wood. "That says two hundred and twenty-

seven, right?"

"Yes." I laugh.

"Then we're here!" His words are more enthusiastic than his actions as he slides his ID through the top of the handle. It takes him two more tries until the light turns green before he pushes down on the handle. "Welcome to mí casa!" He waltzes in but ends up tripping over the navy-blue backpack he left on the floor. He tries to catch himself on his desk chair but misses, forcing me to enter the room.

"Hey now." I wrap my arm around his stomach, while my left arm gets caught under his armpit. I yank my hand out and wipe it on my jeans. "Which bed is yours?"

"This one." He slaps his hand down on the corner of the maroon comforter in front of him.

"Okay." I breathe in, but all I smell is the powdery scent of his cologne. For a second, the roles are reversed. I'm the one intoxicated, but then his feet slip again, and I realize he kicked off his sneakers. I take a step back and let him slide his black sock-covered feet against the wooden floor. He's using the edge of his bed like a toddler learning how to walk while I'm back to fidgeting at my sudden uselessness.

"God, I'm sweating." Trent pushes himself up to a standing position and reaches for the hem of his shirt. It takes another fling of his hand before he's standing in front of me—all tan and shirtless.

I think that's what shocks me the most. We're now closer to winter than summer, yet he's still tan. Also, the way his jeans are hanging dangerously low on his hips. I'm surprised the plaid underwear poking out is just a line.

I'm also surprised I don't get whiplash from how fast my body whips around. I keep my eyes locked on the dry erase board hanging on the door. I now agree with the

sweat statement. My blood feels like it's boiling to the surface of my skin, but I'm nowhere near hot enough to rip my shirt off.

"I blame the Cheetos and Oreos. I love Oreos."

I slowly turn my head around only to see Trent poking his stomach as if he doesn't recognize it.

"Plus, I'm more of a runner than a bench presser."

There's no cheese grate lining his stomach, and he's got more of a half-circle poking out of his jeans than a V. There's something about this candid, in-person, photoshoot-like display that puts any and every single image of a six-pack I've ever seen to shame.

"Whoa." Trent slips again and splays both hands on the side of his bed to steady himself. He stands there to collect himself, or at least I thought he was trying to steady himself until his shoulders start shaking again with laughter.

"Okay," I say for what seems like the millionth time, except this time, I sound more like an annoyed parent. I even go as far as to run my hands through my hair before folding my arms across my chest. That's when I realize we have the same outfit on. The only difference is my long-sleeve shirt is striped with red and blue, and my jeans have a bold navy-blue stripe running down the outer seam of each leg. I take a tentative step forward. "Do you think you can climb in there yourself?"

"Yessir." He whirls around and jumps up.

The mattress squeaks as his butt plops down on the edge, but my mama-bear instincts propel me back over to his side when he almost slips off. My hands hover over his naked upper body before I settle on tentatively pushing his shoulders down. Trent's eyes are burning into my face, but he lets me slowly guide him back. It doesn't take long for him to lean out of my grasp, and I have to shuffle forward,

but this time when I readjust my fingertips against his skin, he flinches.

"*Jeez,* your hands are freezing."

"Sorry." I pull my hands away and go to wipe them on my jeans again, but he yanks my hands back.

"I can warm them up." He sandwiches my hands between his right before his head hits the pillow. His eyelids flutter closed while my hands remain sandwiched between his hands and his chest.

All I can think about is he wasn't kidding about being hot before because his skin is searing compared to mine. As I continue to stand there, awkwardly leaning over him, I can't help but think about the slow thumping of his heart underneath my fingertips.

One heart. Four chambers.

Blood goes into the right atrium, and the right atrium pumps it down to the right ventricle. The right ventricle pumps the blood down to the lungs.

I inhale.

There's the oxygen.

The left atrium receives the oxygenated blood and pumps it to the left ventricle. The left ventricle sends all the oxygenated blood to the rest of the body.

One life beating beneath my fingertips. All red and real and pulsing.

I gently pull my hands away when his chest's up and down movement is in sync with his slowed heart rate. I leave his student ID on his desk and shut the lights off before closing the door shut behind me.

CHAPTER ELEVEN: AND MAYBE DO OTHER THINGS

I hope you know I don't take my shirt off for just anyone.

"Sorry," I mumble to the girl who's holding the door open for me. It's usually a hit or miss when it comes to holding doors. I try to hold the door for other people because I don't like getting hit in the face, but today I almost missed the door because I was too busy staring at my phone.

I step outside after holding the door for the person behind me, but it takes me a few more steps to realize I have this goofy smile on my face. It's not a full-blown, teeth-showing smile, but rather the corners of lips are defying gravity as they reach for the blue sky above me.

I duck my head down and go out of my way to step on a leaf before finally allowing myself to look at my phone again. I usually don't like walking with my face in my screen, but I can't help but respond to Trent's text.

Well, I don't help just any drunk person.

I hike my backpack higher up on my shoulder as I continue walking back to my dorm. It's the coldest day so far, and I'm wearing my black peacoat to prove it. The only problem is the material isn't very backpack friendly. I have

to put more effort in keeping my bag straps at comfortable positions around my shoulders.

Once I'm back in my dorm, I let everything fall from me: my backpack, my coat, and my shoes. I even trade my jeans in for some yoga pants, but I keep my thin purple sweater on. While I should settle in at my desk and attempt to get some work done, I opt for my bed instead. That's when another text finally floats in.

I'm really sorry. I just wanted to shut my brain off.

My fingers hover over my phone screen before I finally begin typing a reply.

I don't like to drink, but I know the feeling.

I spend a few minutes aimlessly scrolling and even nose-laughing at a few funny videos Stephanie sent me since the last time I was on my phone. Stephanie even reciprocates some of my laughing emojis before I get another text from Trent.

How do you shut your brain off then?

Sometimes all I have to do is scroll through my phone. Depending on my mood, I'll either end up neck-deep in some funny videos or sped-up hair tutorials. Today, it is funny videos, and I almost forget to reply to his text.

Idk watch a movie, go for a run, take a nap.

Those things are also true, and I even add a laughing emoji at the end of the sentence because those are the most generic things to do when you don't feel like being "you."

Stephanie gently opens the door, but then seeing I'm awake and not napping, she slams it closed behind her. "My professor needs to take the freaking stick out of his ass before next class; otherwise, I'm not going."

I sit up straighter against my pillows. "What happened?"

"The usual." She grumbles as she tosses her backpack against her desk before jumping up on her bed. "I raise my

hand because he asks for opinions, and no one else likes to give them, yet no matter what I say, he goes against it."

"I'm sorry," I say even though it's the lamest reply in the book.

"It's okay." She runs a hand through her hair. "It's just annoying because he makes me feel so stupid. Like, I know I can be stupid sometimes—"

"You're not stupid."

"No." Stephanie holds her finger up. "I can be stupid, but not when it comes to the more serious stuff, and yet he acts like I don't know anything just because I haven't been teaching it for thirty-plus years."

"That is annoying." It's another lame reply, but I'm too focused on the reply sitting on my phone screen.

That can be arranged.

****

It took until our next philosophy class for Trent to finally elaborate because he decided to respond to my question mark with a *TTYL*.

"How's your workload looking this week?" Is how he started the dialogue before continuing with, "you should come over and watch a movie in my dorm when you're free."

I can't remember if I said "okay" or "sounds good" before we parted ways on the cement-like we always do. It was a completely casual conversation like it always is.

Now it's Thursday night, and the girls won't stop giggling as they walk me across campus to Trent's dorm. We all agreed I shouldn't walk in the dark alone, but with each step closer, that's all I'm starting to feel—all alone with my little cartoon character running around and

around.

This was all so casual. This was all supposed to be so casual, yet Stephanie's voice continues to echo in my head.

"That's code for come over, and let's make out."

"And maybe do other things." Savannah wiggled her eyebrows.

I've been squirming ever since.

It doesn't help that it's cold outside, and all I'm wearing is a long-sleeve shirt and my windbreaker. I opted for my sneakers, but I still couldn't bring myself to put on sweatpants instead of jeans. That would've felt too casual.

Trent looks casual when we finally spot him under the faint orange glow of the lamppost hovering over the cement pathway. He looks almost too casual. All leaned up against the dorm building, grey sweatpants, dark red sweatshirt, and his face tucked into his phone screen.

Maybe I did opt for the right attire since the chill in the air is replaced with warmth the second I lay my eyes on him. My heart has been pounding away this entire time, beating with every step, but as Trent pockets his phone and takes the few steps forward to meet us halfway, it's relentless. *Boom, splat* against the pavement. Any minute now.

"Hey." There go his lips.

My greeting turns into a grunt when a hand slams into the top of my back.

"Bye, Lacie!"

"Have fun!"

"Love you!"

They leave me coughing and chuckling, but I bet the latter was the only goal.

"Sorry." I squeak as I flick my thumb over my shoulder, gesturing to the giggling goons I call friends.

Trent only waves his hand before mimicking my actions. "Want to go inside?"

I hold up my hand. "I think the life of my fingers depends on it."

Trent chuckles as he turns around, but his hand swings up and latches on to mine. The sleeve of his sweatshirt presses into my palm as he tugs me forward. I barely feel or even notice the gesture until we edge closer and closer to his door.

"That's code for come over, and let's make out."

"And maybe do other things."

Trent uses his other hand to slide his ID through before he pushes open his door the same way he did the other day.

"Welcome to mí casa!" He walks in and spreads his arms out before dropping his hands back down. "Again." He goes over to his bed and starts moving around his pillows and straightening his comforter. "Zack's at a club meeting, so we won't be bothered, and I promise all my blankets are clean." He lifts the screen of the silver laptop resting on the end of the bed. "But we're going to have to suffer with my small laptop screen. I have a small selection of DVDs, but I figured we could just use Netflix." He unzips his sweatshirt with just one swoosh of his hand, and that solidifies my frozen state.

It doesn't help that he was all tan and shirtless the last time I was here. I was too distracted then to even take a good look around. Half of the room is divided between Trent and Zack the same way mine is divided between Stephanie and me, but while we both try to keep our stuff from spilling into each other's, their stuff seems to overlap. All the different patterned vans under Zack's bed spill out into the middle, while Trent has a little nightstand under the window with a lamp and other electronic devices and

plugs.

"All my blankets are clean."

"We won't be bothered."

"And maybe do other things."

"So." Trent jumps up on his bed like he did the other day, only this time he makes it to the center. "I know horror movies are out." He drags his computer onto his lap as he settles his back against his pillows before he glances back up. "Oh, that's basil, by the way." Trent nods to the fish tank I was eyeing on Zack's desk.

"Hi, Basil." The dark blue beta fish wiggles around. It freezes as if locking eyes with me before going back on its merry way around one of the little decorative plants. My eyes are like a moth to flame on the blue light illuminating the tank, but I think it has more to do with the eyes burning into the side of my head than any actual instinctual attraction. "Oh, um, yes." I pass a glance his way. "Anything but horror, please."

Trent smiles a little as he starts clicking around. I slowly kick off my shoes and inch further into the space. My eyes read some of the band names and musical playbills Zack has collaged over his bedside. Trent only has a miniature basketball hoop hanging over the side of his bed.

I almost want to cringe as I slowly peel my jacket off and gently hang it on his desk chair because now I also have Stephanie and Savannah's cartoon characters running around inside my head. They're gushing about how movies lead to kissing, which leads to taking clothes off. Of course, I've thought about it before, but thinking about it is a lot different than doing it, which is why I continue moving. Objects in motion tend to stay in motion. It's one of the only things I ever grasped from physics. Objects at rest tend to stay at rest, the only other thing I grasped and what

pops into my head when I finally sit down next to Trent.

The mattress creaks and my hands are wringing together, but my spine goes rigid when I feel Trent's eyes once again burning into the side of my head.

"Lacie?" he asks.

"Yeah?" I keep my eyes glued to his laptop screen.

"We have a problem."

My shoulders finally slump down into a cringe. "Why?"

"Because I like to cuddle, and this—" He gestures to the chunk of space I put between us. "Isn't going to cut it."

"But I—" I pause as my hand flings between us. "It's awkward."

"What?" Trent sputters before he reaches across his legs and yanks up a grey fuzzy blanket. "Then you've been cuddling with the wrong people."

"I'm serious."

"So am I." He holds his laptop up with one hand while spreading the blanket over our legs with the other.

My fingers begin wrestling again while Trent continues to tuck the blanket around his legs and snuggle further down against his pillows.

"Okay, now you come over here." Trent's hand slowly slides around the curve of my back, and he uses it to gently coax me closer to his side and further down against the pillows. "See?" Both his hands go back to clicking against the keys. "Now—" He passes a glance in my direction before quickly flicking the blanket up a little higher, so it's finally over my shoulders. "Now we're all cozy."

Trent's head is the only thing poking out of the blanket. If it weren't for the light stubble on his jaw, he could be mistaken for a little kid all tucked up. Especially when he finally turns his head and blinks back at me with his eyes

all wide and innocent.

"Comedy?" he asks.

"Comedy." I nod.

He scrolls around for a few more minutes before clicking on the newest one, and I finally allow my body to sag against his comforter.

****

The white-lettered credits roll across the black screen for a few seconds before Trent clicks pause.

"What?" he asks.

"What?" I echo.

"You're making a face." Trent's shoulders shake as he attempts to hold in his laughter.

I finally stop wrinkling my nose. "Sorry." I squirm before running a hand through my hair. "I don't know how I feel."

"Same." The mattress dips a little as Trent wiggles his way up to match my sitting position. "I feel like they could have done better."

"Right?" I nod. "Like, the beginning was good, but then it lost its momentum."

"Yeah." Trent scratches his jaw. "I feel like all the jokes were in the beginning."

"And the rest were forced." I continue while I hear some mumbling outside Trent's door. A consistent "dun dun dun dun" that gets louder and louder until the door slams open and the dry erase board on the back goes clattering to the floor.

"Zack Attack!" Zack chants with his arms stretched out in front of him. He uses them as pretend jaws, clapping them together in the air. He finally drops his arms back

down when he's only met with our silence and takes the time to flick his head, flicking the brown hair off his forehead.

"I think sharks have a more upward bite. You know, with just the lower jaws moving. That was more of an alligator." I can't help but throw in my two cents, anything to cover the silence, while Trent sputters again.

Zack shakes his head as he kicks off his black and white checkered vans. "Science Majors."

CHAPTER TWELVE: THERE'S A DIFFERENCE

"And there stands a lone pea."

I don't bother shaking my head or rolling my eyes. I stare back at Zack as he continues to trot away from me on the sidewalk. Correction: as he continues to grin and happily slap his feet against the pavement.

"I would ask what your favorite thing to eat for Thanksgiving is, but..." He throws his hands up in a shrug. Trent reaches up and whacks the back of his head. Or at least he attempts to, but Zack only gets a scrape to the neck because of both his extra few inches in height and his intuition to cower away. "My favorite is mashed potatoes in case anyone is wondering." Zack continues once he makes it to the passenger side of Trent's small black car.

I can only bring myself to wrinkle my nose as the wind whips my ponytail around, and my fingers continue to curl around my small duffel bag.

"You don't like mashed potatoes?" Zack's yell makes me laugh as I shake my head. I hear Trent's gasp before his head pops back up from behind the trunk.

"And I was even going to offer you a ride." Trent shakes his head.

Zack mimics his actions as he chews on a strand of red licorice.

"Seriously, though." Trent continues after slamming his

trunk closed and walking over to the driver's side of the car. "Are you sure you don't need a ride? I mean, we go to the same grocery store, so you must live pretty close."

My eyebrows rise. I can't decide whether to take him seriously or make a joke about stalking. I guess Trent begins conjuring up the latter as he reaches up to scratch the back of his neck.

"You know what I mean," Trent offers, but now Zack's shaking his head at him as he continues to pull candy out of his navy-blue puffy vest pocket.

People continue to zip into and out of their cars and into and out of the parking lot. I'm sure my nose is red, and my fingers are almost numb, but it's all worth it when my mom's van pulls up to the curb. She rolls down the passenger window.

"There's my girl!" She waves me in before using that same arm to squish me in a side hug as she plants a kiss on my head. "Who was that?"

"Oh." I forgot all about Zack and— "Just Trent."

"Just Trent." She hums.

"Mmhm." I crane my neck back. "Whatcha reading, Lay?"

Her head flies up so fast she has to adjust her bangs, but a smile stretches across her face. "It's a slow part right now, but the next scene..." She talks us through the first hour of the drive, which is perfect because she loves any opportunity to break down cute scenes, while I'd love to avoid giving my mom a plot summary.

****

As soon as I got home, I threw on my favorite pajamas, plopped down on the couch with my fluffiest blanket, and

have only moved to chow down one of my favorite dinners: penne alla vodka. No restaurant compares to how my parents make it, even though my parents constantly ask who makes it better between them.

Layla's propped up on the one-person couch with her blanket and book in her lap. She's up to *A Bend in the Road.* My dad is stretched out across the two-person couch on my left while my mom is curled up on the other end of the couch beside me. All of us have our faces buried in our own technological devices, but we still have the television on because we still can't decide what movie to watch.

I hope this isn't weird, but I didn't know you had a sister.

I wait a minute before typing back a reply.

Yeah, sorry I never said goodbye.

Don't be sorry. Trent's reply floats in on top of my aimless scrolling. *I wish my family was that excited to see me.* I flick the messages away to finish the video I'm watching, and another text floats in as soon as I finish. *Actually, my dog is, and he enjoys cuddling with me.*

Do you have any siblings?

Technically yes, two half-brothers. A beat passes before he adds. *Both older and rag on me constantly lol.*

I glance up to find my sister staring back at me.

"What?" I ask when she doesn't stop.

"Why are you smiling?"

That's when I feel it. My lips are trying to defy gravity. I try to downplay it, but my mom turns her head. Her eyebrows go down in curiosity before they shoot back up, and she throws me an all-too-knowing smile that Stephanie would be proud of.

****

Finals are officially on the horizon. I mean, they've always been there, sitting at the end of each syllabus, but now they're burning bright like the rising sun. Highlighted on paper, in my planner, and in my phone.

With each class I go to, I'm only dumped with more test dates, study guides and topics, final reading assignments, and paper questions. I'm trying not to freak out, but that doesn't mean I haven't already called my mom on the verge of overthinking, prestressing panic. Of course, she said I'll be fine, it'll be over before I know it, and I'll be home before I know it—all reassuring and motivational.

It also helps that I'm still learning new things in my classes. The new things keep my mind distracted, my pen moving across my notebooks, and finals in the near future where they belong.

However, Trent's leg has been bouncing up and down for the last forty minutes.

Okay, that's an exaggeration.

There have been a few intermissions, but they have been few and far between. And it's all distracted me from Professor Collins' words.

I've dwindled it down to two things.

The reality of finals has also dawned on him, or he has to pee.

"All right, we've got two more readings on Aristotle to go through next week. Then, we review. Any questions?" Professor Collins holds out his hands as his beady eyes scan over the room. When all he receives is silence and blank stares, he claps his hands back together. "Go eat."

I take his words as permission to finally flip my notebook closed, while Trent's knee takes them as permission to start bouncing again. It doesn't last long because soon, he's standing up and pushing in his seat. I

follow suit and begin trudging up the platform-like steps, but his hand flies next to my head to catch the door from the girl ahead of us.

"So, that was brutal."

"Yeah." I nod. "It dragged a little today."

Feet scrape and squeak against the hallway as everyone heads for the exits. We walk out the same exit we always do before stopping at the far edge of the cement pathway where we always stop. Only today, Trent teeters on the grass a little.

"So, I was wondering—" he scratches the back of his neck. "I mean, I know timing may be tight with classes ending soon and finals, but—" Trent moves his head to block the sun I've been squinting at, and we trade smiles for a second before he's back to teetering. "But, um, so I was wondering if you wanted to—"

"Yo, Trent!"

Trent's sneakers finally sink into the grass as he whirls around. There is a group—actually no—a gaggle—of guys hanging out on the cement pathway on the left. Trent flicks his hand up in a wave, but that only promotes their whistles and catcalling. They're lingering near the same large patch of grass we're on the edge of, like a group of geese.

"Sorry, uh, I was just wondering if—"

"Trent!" One guy yells.

The other people walking by whip their heads around, but they all continue to laugh.

Trent looks torn as he lifts his bag strap higher up on his shoulders. "I'm sorry about—" He waves his hand before taking a step closer. "Do you want to go out, um, with me?"

"*Go out.*" Not "hang out." There's a difference, and my internal sirens are blaring.

"You know." Trent scratches his jaw before pulling at the skin there. "Before we go on break."

"Okay." I hear myself say before I shake my head. "I mean, yes."

Trent froze as soon as I opened my mouth, but now I watch as the muscles he has pinched between his fingers curl up to reveal his teeth.

"Okay." He breathes before finally dropping his hand. "Cool." He stuffs his hands in his sweatpants pockets and flashes me with a full smile as he steps back. "I'll text you."

I check behind me before mimicking the step. "Okay."

Trent keeps smiling and nods as he takes another step back. I send him my version of his usual tipped-up lips as I take another step. Then, we both duck, turn, and go our separate ways. Only then do I finally allow a full-blown smile to grace my lips. A smile I don't care who happens to see.

CHAPTER THIRTEEN: VANILLA VELVET

"Would you stop pacing? You're creating a draft." Stephanie waves her hand in the air.

I'm mid-stride, but my hands continue to wrestle each other.

The roles are reversed on this parallel universe Friday night. Stephanie's the one curled up in her bed while I'm dressed to go out, specifically, dressed to "go out" with Trent. I keep telling myself it's just another "hang out" since we are only meeting at the student center again, and it's only a little after dinner time. Still, I can't stop thinking about the way his leg kept bouncing the other day as if he also knew it was going to be different, and my heart has been bouncing ever since.

"Stop fidgeting." Stephanie doesn't even glance up. "You look fine."

Another difference between the two of us—Stephanie's usually all cool and collected, while here I am all shaky and sweaty. My hair keeps getting in my lip gloss, and I keep pushing it out of the way. But each time I run my fingers through it, I'm reminded of the few pimples crowded around my left temple. I probably created them with the constant habit.

"—psychopath."

"What?" I whirl around to find Stephanie with her

finger pointed in the air like Professor Collins mid-way through a speech.

"I took a Forensics class in high school, so I was saying that the chances of Trent turning into some crazy person ten years from now are pretty high, but right now, he should be fine."

I contemplate her words. "That's oddly reassuring... sort of."

Stephanie triumphantly slumps back down against her pillows while I go back to fidgeting only a little more discreetly. I settle on just literally twiddling my thumbs.

I left my phone on my bed and watch as the black screen lights up.

On my way be there in a few minutes.

"Then again, college guys can be unpredictable."

"What was that?"

"Nothing." She continues scrolling through her phone with her curls all splayed out beside her head.

I catch a glimpse of myself in the small, silver circle mirror on her desk. I used it to apply mascara before but also found myself flipping it around to the magnified side. Every eyebrow hair, pour, and acne scar was visible—too visible, but I couldn't bring myself to apply more makeup because it's only Trent.

I also never really add anything to my hair except for some leave-in conditioner and mousse, but today Megan added a few more waves to it with her curling iron. My hair is leaning more towards wavy as opposed to its half-wavy, half-straight self. For now, at least, if I can bring myself to stop running my hands through it.

Because it's just Trent.

Before I flipped the mirror back around, I relaxed against the back of Stephanie's desk chair and stared back

at myself.

"It makes your eyes pop." She had approved of the army green sweater I threw on, and I embraced the compliment at that moment even though Trent's eyes are still greener, like some unexplainable electricity. Clear. Charge to three hundred. Shock delivered. They blaze and sizzle. Even when his shoulders are slumped with exhaustion and his eyelids droop, his irises still remain crackling.

But he's still Trent.

At least, that's what I keep reminding myself as I finally throw on my black peacoat and when I slip on my black moccasin slippers as opposed to boots.

"Okay." I slip my cross-body bag over one shoulder with one hand while gripping my phone in the other. "Wish me luck."

"Good luck!" Stephanie calls. "Text me if you need anything. You know some snacks, a condom—"

"Not funny!" My hand practically flies away from the door handle.

"I'm kidding." She cackles at the ceiling before flinging her body up. "Seriously, you can text me if you need. Especially if he starts to give you creepy serial killer vibes."

"Will do." I nod.

She waves her hand. "Now go on—get out of here, or am I going to have to push you out?"

"You might." I laugh as I reach for the door handle again. My fingers quiver a little, but I push down on the handle, pushing down any of my remaining hesitation. "Bye, crazy!"

"Have fun!" she singsongs.

I catch one final glimpse of her in between the crack in the door. She sticks her tongue out. I mimic the expression before a smile takes over my face as the door clicks closed

behind me.

****

I picked the end of another rectangular table with my back facing the food counters. I don't know if it's my stomach, my heart, or maybe even one of my kidneys stuffed up in my throat. Either way, I feel full there and hollow everywhere else as I press send on the text.

I'm here.

Luckily, there's only leftover dinner commotion with a few people scattered around. Some are in small groups, some in pairs, and most are accompanied by just their notebooks or laptops, probably studying for finals.

The chatter grows and then softens every few minutes with minimal laughter in between, but it all sounds loud to me. It all only reminds me of the empty seat across from me.

"Yo! Look who it is."

I hear some back slaps and handshakes.

"How are you, my man?"

"Yeah, bro. What's happening?"

"Nothin' much." Just two words mumbled out from the very back of Trent's throat where your esophagus meets your tongue, where your vocal cords break out into the softest vibrations. He's at the other end of the room, at the entrance of the food center, but it feels like he's right in front of me, and my throat feels like it's closing again.

"Whatcha got there?"

I hear some rustling of plastic bags.

"Oh, nothing." There he goes again.

"Ah-ha, well, you should come down to B-three."

"Yeah, buddy, Swansons' got the hookup."

I can only picture the way Trent's shoulders shake as he chuckles. "Maybe later."

"All right, man." This guy purposely drags out the words. "All right."

There are a few more heavy back claps before sneakers and work boots squeak and scuff against the linoleum floor.

I keep my eyes glued to my phone screen. I didn't even realize Trent responded to my text with an *on my way*.

"Hey," Trent says as he gently places a white plastic grocery bag on the table. "Sorry for taking so long."

He shrugs off his black fleece jacket. He also decided to wear a sweater and jeans. Only his sweater is black and hugs his chest, while mine is tight around the arms and loose everywhere else.

"So." He rubs his hands together before both his eyebrows quirk up. "You ready?"

I mimic the expression only in hesitation. "For what?"

Trent only smiles as he reaches into the grocery bag. "I thought we could try each other's flavors." He wiggles his eyebrows but then freezes. "Not like that, I swear."

I can't help but laugh. Clear, charge to three hundred, and it finally feels like I can breathe again—at least a little bit. "It's okay."

"Good." His chest expands on an inhale before he reaches into the plastic bag again. He pulls out a plastic container filled with twelve mini vanilla cupcakes and a wider container with only six large red velvet cupcakes. "Sadly, cupcakes were the best I could do."

My lips curl together. "You can't tell me you've never had a vanilla cupcake before."

Trent rolls his head back along with his eyes. "You know what I mean."

He pulls some brown napkins out of the bag and passes me one before cracking open the containers. We both reach our hands out but retract them when we realize our trajectory is in the same direction. The process repeats, and we both pull back sheepishly.

"You go," Trent offers.

"No, you."

We both reach out again, and our fingers bump together. We both look up, our lips stretching into similar smiles, before we finally maneuver our arms, crisscrossing them over each other. I make sure the icing on the red velvet cupcake I choose isn't smudged against the side of the container, while Trent doesn't hesitate in reaching for any vanilla one.

"So," he says as he begins peeling the semi-clear wrapper off the bottom. The mini cupcake looks even smaller, perched between his fingertips. "Got any plans over break?"

"Honestly, I haven't let myself think about it. I've been more focused on getting through finals."

Trent jokingly shakes his head. "They're not that bad. Don't believe the internet."

"I know." I breathe out a laugh. "But if I already think about being able to do nothing over break, then I'll stop doing stuff now."

Trent covers his mouth as he chuckles, but I start laughing again when I realize he stuffed the entire cupcake into his mouth. His shoulders shake as he holds his finger up and picks up a napkin.

I finally finish flattening the wrapper around the regular-sized cupcake in front of me and stick my finger into the icing.

"I have a question," I say before licking the icing off my

finger. "If we never met in the grocery store, would you still think my favorite flavor is vanilla?"

Trent has another vanilla cupcake perched between his fingers and pauses halfway through unwrapping it. "Yes."

I slam my hands down so hard that the table rattles. "Really? No way." My mouth opens and closes a few times. "But why?"

Trent's shoulders shake as he attempts to lick the icing off his lips. He ends up having to put the cupcake down and grabs another napkin.

"Because," he finally says as he leans forward. He uses his pointer finger to draw a slow circle around me. "Everything about you just sort of screams…vanilla." He picks the cupcake back up. "Plus, you use vanilla perfume and whatnot." He goes to take a bite, but his eyes dart back up. "It's not a bad thing."

"It sounds like a bad thing." I'm starting to have more than just a cupcake in my throat again.

"It's not." Trent laughs.

I press my lips together as I stare back at him. "I don't believe you."

"It's really not." He goes to bite into the cupcake again but then decides against it. "Okay fine." He places the cupcake down and sits up straighter. "What about me? What flavor would you have used to describe me?"

I wait until I finish chewing before shrugging. "Chocolate."

Trent's eyebrows shoot all the way up to his hairline, but he pursues even more theatrics by splaying a hand across his chest. "Really? Plain old chocolate?" He throws in a pout. "I'm wounded."

"But red velvet technically is—"

"Don't." He holds his finger up. "Don't even go there."

My lips continue to quake with my amusement. "What's so special about red velvet then?"

He cups his pointer finger and thumb around his jaw as he leans back—more theatrics. I'm surprised no one's noticed. Then again, this may be the longest time he's gone by in public without a catcall or shout-out.

"Well, red is my favorite color." He finally drops his hand. "And velvet isn't just soft, but rather smooth." He runs his hand over the air as if he's metaphorically feeling it, and his lips are all pinched together in some kind of cigar dangling smolder. I don't know what the puppeteer is thinking today, but I do know my laugh is way too loud for the people around us. Thankfully, I finished my cupcake because my head falls forward way too fast, and the last thing I need is a face full of icing.

"Now I have to have one." Trent's hand darts out for a red velvet cupcake, and I sit back up in time to catch him peeling off the wrapper. "Okay," he says after placing the now naked cupcake down on his napkin. "Same question." He goes to run his fingers through his hair, hesitates, checks his fingers for icing, and then proceeds. He goes to rest his hands in his lap but decides to fold them in front of him. "Why vanilla?" I raise my eyebrows at him, making his lips quiver, but he keeps up the now therapist act. "I'm listening." He throws out his hand before curling his fingers together again.

I shake my head as I reach for a vanilla cupcake and pick the little round pastel sprinkles off with my fingers. I can hear my family cringing at me inside my head as I eat them.

"The way I see it," I say after wiping my fingers on my napkin. "Vanilla is like the base of all the other flavors." I begin peeling down the wrapper. "You know, you add

cocoa to vanilla to get chocolate. You can add any fruit to vanilla, and it becomes that flavor. You are essentially always starting with the same ingredients, with vanilla, and then only adding things to it. The same way oxygen is needed to make carbon dioxide and water and glucose and—a bunch of other things."

My spine goes stiff at the fact that I just willingly mentioned chemistry, and all Trent seems to be doing is blinking back at me. I ruined the moment for sure. I ran it over with my big mouth. Plus, I finished all the sprinkles, so I have nothing left to do with my fingers.

I wrack my brain for something—anything else to say to fill the silence, but instead, my eyes catch on to the all too familiar lopsided curve that is Trent's light pink lips. The theatrics ensue as he sighs through his nose and leans his head on his hand.

"I love when you talk science to me."

I shove a big chunk of icing in my mouth to prevent from smiling, but I fail. I fail big time.

CHAPTER FOURTEEN: STUDY SESSION
PART I

Some plants have seeds, and some don't.

Trent's pen is blue, and he's got a swatch of it on the side of his hand from dragging it against his notebook page.

Plants that don't make seeds and have no roots, stems, or leave structures are algae.

Trent twirls his pen between his fingertips. He tucks it under and over his first three fingers before swinging it back.

Plants that don't make seeds and have some structures are moss. Plants that don't make seeds but have structure are ferns.

Trent places the end of his pen between his lips.

Plants that have seeds, but no flowers are conifers. Plants that have seeds and flowers are flowers.

Trent tips his head ever so slightly in my direction. His pen is still pressed up against his lips as his eyes burn into the side of my head.

I don't move my head. I just use my eyes to look up at him.

He looks away.

Back to the plant kingdom.

Repeat.

Trent's actions are easier to memorize than my homework. They always are. A pen twirl, pen to lip, a glance, and repeat. A jaw scratch, a neck scratch, an arm or leg stretch, and repeat.

"It will be fun," they said. By they, I mean, Trent said, when he first suggested that we should have study sessions on the floor of his dorm room in preparation for finals. "I won't distract you." He promised. "Pretty please." His eyes sparkled in the sunlight as he pouted at me. I blame that pout. At this rate, it will be the death of my education. All my grades are about to be flushed down the toilet all because of that pout.

"I have a question."

I don't bother looking up. "I have an answer."

"If you could switch bodies with anyone or anything for one whole day, would you do it?"

My pen drops. "Really?"

"What?"

"That's not the philosophy we need to be worried about right now."

He chuckles. "I know, but you hate it that much?"

"No, not hate just…" I pull my lips together as I try not to reciprocate his smile. His amusement is contagious like an invasive plant species. "Okay, yeah, because sometimes science—" I use my thighs to lift up my textbook "—is easier."

"Point taken." He tilts his head as if to make an invisible tally mark in the air. "But you still didn't answer my question."

I mockingly roll my eyes. "My sister, I guess."

"You guess?"

"Yeah." I laugh. "I want to know what it's like inside

her brain. Plus, it would be nice to be the younger sibling for a change."

"It sucks."

"Better than doing everything first."

"I don't know." He sings the words but takes a second to rub his face. "I end up getting stuck doing everything anyway. Plus," he leans over and passes a glance at all the black pen ink covering my notebook, "you always seem like you have it all together."

"Yeah, okay." My eyes roll up to the ceiling while my hand still splays across my notebook, covering all my chicken scratch. "What about you?"

"Me? I'd have to think about that." He outlines his chin with his pointer finger and thumb, making a checkmark, and purses his lips as if he's smoking on a pipe.

I gently push on his shoulder. "You're such a weirdo."

He sobers up. "No, that would be Zack."

"Sure," I drag out the word.

"Believe me, I know, which is why I wouldn't switch bodies with him. I'd never been able to get the show tunes out of my head or the country music."

"Uh, uh, uh." I wag my finger. "Zack said you're the one with the country music obsession."

His mouth drops. "Lies."

My laughter bounces off the walls. "I don't think so."

"Lies, I say, lies." He reaches over and tickles my sides.

"Okay, okay!" I squeal and try to shoo him away without bending the pages of my notebook. Too bad he rips it from my hands.

"Clear!" He jokes before pretending to zap my sides with electric wires.

"Stop!" I continue to laugh. He really is the weirdo. I would never have guessed. One minute he's slouched

down in a hoodie in the back of a lecture hall, and the next, he's pulling cartoon voices and tickling me.

He lets me sit back up after a few seconds as his chuckles fade.

"You're so distracting." I huff as I tug at my sweatshirt and fix my hair.

"Sorry." He continues to chuckle to himself. "I'll stop." He holds his hand up as if taking a vow. "Scouts honor."

"Boy scouts? That's your wolf pack?"

"Mmhm." His pen is back in his mouth.

I curl my legs back up in a pretzel position and return to my plants. All flora, no fauna. Native and non-native. Invasive and non-invasive. Trent goes back to pen twirling and reading, or maybe even pretending to read at this point. I'll never know, but my eyes flicker up to find his teeth surrounding his pen this time as he's looking at me— a nervous stretch of teeth.

"What?" I ask.

"Nothing." His eyes dart away, but then he almost drops his pen. "I just have another question." He looks back. "A serious one this time, promise."

"Okay." I nod as I go back to scribbling more stuff down. A few seconds pass with only the wind blowing against the window outside before Trent shifts on the grey fuzzy blanket.

"Do you believe in all this?"

"All this…"

"This education, I mean?"

"Do you believe that there are almost four hundred thousand plant species?"

A ghost of a smile traces his lips, but he tugs it away with his thumb and continues to stare at the notebook perched on his outstretched legs.

I have to blink away pictures of moss and algae as I sit up straighter. "On the good days." I sigh. "But sometimes it's overwhelming, all the information. It makes me feel like a bobblehead."

"Do you—" He twists his torso around but hesitates. "Do you believe mental health is just as important as physical health?"

"Of course."

"Same!" Trent stuffs his hand into his hair.

I turn the textbook page and continue skimming for all the information I need to refresh myself on.

"But the other day, my professor he—he kind of brushed me off about it. At least when it comes to little kids."

I slowly lift my head to reveal the gaping hole that is now my mouth.

Trent's lips curl up again, but he's quick to shake his head. "I don't know. It was weird." He shifts back around and picks up his laptop. "That's why I asked the other question. Things like that make me question all of this." He picks at the grey fuzzy blanket underneath us. The same little fuzzies are stuck to my black leggings. "Makes me feel like a bobblehead." He mimics my head shake but throws in some extra arm flails. I shove his shoulder, so his head bobbles even more.

If he were a bobblehead or even a cartoon character, I think this would be his outfit anyway—T-shirt and sweatpants. Today, the specific variation is a grey t-shirt and black sweatpants, but I also happen to be wearing a similar get-up. The only difference is my white socks have flowers on them.

Trent uses the blanket to slide his backpack closer.

My eyes land on my backpack beside me and the words

on my notebook that I'm supposed to be absorbing before I turn my head back over to him. "You know, I think the problem is we tend to oversimplify complex things and make simple things too complex."

Trent's eyebrows rise above his water bottle. "Who's the philosophical one now?"

"I'm serious." I laugh. "But you started it."

The amusement shines in his eyes as he shrugs and continues drinking, so I continue spilling all the thoughts I've been thinking since I got my midterm grade for philosophy.

"It's just—I don't know. I feel like we're always searching for two sides instead of seeing that there's multiple. Like when testing a hypothesis." I twist my body around to face him. "The most annoying part of lab write-ups is the evaluation before the conclusion. I mean, yeah, it's because it's more work, but in a way, it's also because none of us like to admit where we went wrong or where things can be flawed. We don't like taking blame. Also, the whole point of the evaluation is to show that there's always more to research and more to learn. Things are always changing, and so are perspectives, and the problem is when they don't. Then the sides come back, and people rather grab their pitchforks than talk to each other. At least, in my opinion. But then again, it's not that simple!" I throw my hands up as I breathe a laugh through my nose.

The silence that follows is expected. My big mouth did it again, went eighty miles per hour in a thirty-mile zone. I blew past all the red lights and stop signs.

I reach back for my ponytail out of habit but quickly drop my hand back down. Trent leans forward. It's as if my fingers stretched out across Trent's face and zoomed right in on his forehead. His eyebrows rise again, and I'm

able to count the four big wrinkles that stretch out across his forehead before he tips his head down.

The air gets caught in the back of my throat as his lips hover over mine. He pushes his hand into the ground beside me and presses his lips against mine just enough to seal my eyelids closed. My heart drums in my ears before Trent pulls back—my exhale becomes his inhale. Those green eyes lock with mine and then flick down again. My eyes are stuck on those baby pink lips of his before they fall on mine again.

My hands fly up to catch his ears and his head as it continues to lean down and down and down while his hands find my waist again. Only this time, they slide back and hold me close as my head leans up and up and up. Plants need oxygen for photosynthesis to create glucose to survive. I'm no longer convinced I need oxygen. I need Trent and his soft lips closer and closer and closer.

Trent seems to be having a similar dilemma because even as his hands fall away and his chest pulls back, it still takes him another extra second to pull his lips away from mine—enough for us to catch our breath. It's enough for the heat pounding through our veins to sear across our cheeks. It's enough for me to see another beautiful upward stretch of his teeth. *Who needs photosynthesis?*

Trent's eyebrows quirk up, making me laugh, but now I feel hot everywhere as if I were the green leaf of a plant turned up to face the brightly burning sun.

"Photosynthesis?" He adds more fuel to the amused fire in his eyes.

I gently push at his shoulder. "Stop distracting me."

He chuckles as he moves back into an upright position. It doesn't take long for his pen to be back in his left hand and his gaze to return to his computer screen.

I readjust my textbook and notebook in my lap and scoot back against the pillows Trent laid out. My eyes continue to dart to the disheveled, dark grey handprint resting on the blanket beside my thigh. Trent's gaze follows mine. His teeth sink into his lower lip as his hand flings up and grabs the back of his neck. We trade nervous stretches of teeth before looking back down at our homework, but neither of us move to erase it. Even if we did, it's still forever imprinted in my brain and seared across my lips.

CHAPTER FIFTEEN: STUDY SESSION PART II

It's another Sunday. I can see the reflection of my fingers typing away on the word document, and I pause to tug at my lip. I catch Stephanie's shadow also reflecting in my laptop screen. She continues to push her hand off her desk and spin her chair around and around.

My phone lights up beside me. I purposely put it on silent to keep it from distracting me, but I don't hesitate to pick it up since HOME is flashing across the top of the screen.

"Hello?"

"Hi, lima bean! Just checking in!"

"Hey, mom."

There's some pounding before my mom sighs. "How are you doing?"

"I'm all right. Just—"

Some more pounding. "Will you stop?"

"You're not doing it right." I hear my dad mumble.

"Go away," my mom says as the pounding ensues.

"You're not supposed to pound half of it."

There's a slam.

"There's no right way to pound chicken!"

Stephanie stops spinning and pierces me with a look. I send her a sheepish smile over my shoulder.

"Mom?" I ask when only more rustling ensues on her

end.

"Yes, bean, sorry, I'm here. Your dad's just being a butthead."

"But you're not—"

"Do you want to make it?"

I let out a laugh because it feels like I'm sitting there at the kitchen table. My heart tugs a little at the thought—just two more weeks.

"Hi, Lacie!" My dad sounds closer to the phone.

"Hi, dad!"

"Go make yourself useful and chop the tomatoes." My mom orders him, and I laugh again as I imagine the hip bump she probably gives him in the direction.

"What are you guys making?" I ask as I prop my feet up and wrap my arm around my legs.

"Oh, just some grilled chicken and then some pasta sauce and meatballs for the week," she says it like it's no big deal, but I would kill to have her and my dad's food right now. After living on diner hall food, I realize I've been spoiled all my life with fresh home-cooked meals, and I vow never to take them for granted again.

"Hold on, Lace, I'm putting you on speaker." I hear a click. "Okay, so anything new?"

I wait a few seconds at the sound of rushing water before responding. "No, not really."

"When are your finals?" my mom asks.

"I have my first final next week for my bio-lab class." I sigh. "I'm finishing my last lab now."

"I feel like that's all you ever do."

My dad barks out a laugh in the background, and I can picture the whole scene. My mom's dark blonde hair twisted up in a claw clip as she still wears her black uniform from her day shift, while my dad still prances around in his

pajamas, more worried about the food he's going to bring with him on his night shift than if his light blue scrubs are even clean.

I hear a slam as something heavy hits the ground. "My teachers are so stupid."

"Layla." My mom's warning is now directed at her.

"What? It's the truth."

"We've discussed this."

"Homework is stupid, too."

"Why is it stupid?" my dad offers.

"I hate math and history and science. It's all stupid."

"Layla." My mom warns again.

"But why?" my dad asks.

"You wouldn't understand."

"Try me."

"No, you wouldn't understand."

"Why not?"

"Because your almost fifty, just like my stupid teacher."

"Layla!" my mom yells.

I can't help but snort. "She's not wrong."

"Hey, now," my dad says, but he sounds like he's trying to hold in a laugh.

"And I bet you're wearing your doggy pajamas."

"Lacie!" My mom's laughing more than yelling now while I bark out a laugh. No pun intended. Actually, pun totally intended because those navy blue, sweater-wearing dog pajamas sum up my dad's very existence: that and his salt and pepper beard.

"Lacie's on the phone? Lacie!" Layla's scream makes me jerk the phone away from my ear, and Stephanie stops spinning again, but she reaches for her large light pink water bottle.

"Hey!" I hear my parents yell, but a new kind of

pounding ensues, but this time it's the pounding of Layla's footsteps before I hear a door slam. "Why are condoms made of rubber?"

Stephanie spits the water she just chugged all over the floor between us, making me burst into laughter.

"My health teacher wouldn't tell me. What's the point of learning about reproductive health in health class if she's not going to answer none of my questions?"

"But why?" I'm coughing along with Stephanie, only she's all red-faced and glossy-eyed, while my shoulders are still shaking with laughter.

"I told her I'm not stupid because, in all of Nicolas Spark's books, the characters have sex. I just want to know why condoms work if they are only made of rubber. She yelled at me and told me that it's not an appropriate question. Then I said, why do all the movies show kids practicing putting condoms on bananas and cucumbers in school? She told me to ask my parents, and I said no, I'm asking you. Then everyone was laughing, so she sent me to the nurse."

"The nurse?"

"The nurse asked why I was there, and I said because I asked Mrs. DeAngelo why condoms are made of rubber, so then she told me to go back to class, and now I'm asking you."

"Did you try Googling it?"

"Duh, I'm not stupid."

"I know." I shake my head even though she can't see. Stephanie still seems to be in shock. "Do you know?" I mouth to her as a joke, and her eyes widen.

"No!"

"All Google said was the malleability of latex and protection from STIs."

"How old is she?" Stephanie whispers.

I sputter. "Twelve. Almost thirteen."

"And they're only ninety-eight percent effective, which means there is a two percent chance of being ineffective, so why do they still make them if they aren't at least one-hundred percent effective?"

"You have to account for." I pause because the phrase I've been told my entire life in science classes, and especially now in my lab class, is now all too ironic. "Human error."

There's a pause, which means she's thinking. "I hate that."

I laugh. "Me too."

"Boys are stupid."

"Ha." Stephanie's back to spinning. "Tell me about it."

"Except for Nicolas Sparks."

"Of course." My eyes catch the ceiling. "Go do your stupid homework."

"Don't tell me what to do."

Three beeps echo in my ear, which means she ended the call.

"Please tell me when your sister is of legal drinking age," Stephanie says. "Because I wanna party with her."

"Be my guest." I laugh, but little does she know I'm laughing more at the fact that Layla would probably never be caught dead in an actual club.

My phone pings again, and, as if on cue, Stephanie slowly spins around to face me like an evil villain on their thrown.

"Let me guess," she says, which she doesn't even have to say, nor does she even need to guess. "The cute boy beckons."

"Stop," I say as I start packing up my things. "We do

homework."

"Yeah, okay."

"We do."

"Have fun." She starts spinning again. "But not too much fun."

I sling my bag over my shoulder. "We're just studying."

"Whatever you say." She hums and throws a wink my way as she turns. She makes it sound so simple. Little does she know that before Trent, all I've had are far away glances, notes thrown in the trash, mumbles about being childish, and daydreams that amounted to nothing. It's like when someone waves to you, and you wave back only to realize they were never even waving to you in the first place.

****

"Hey," Trent whispers. "Hey, Lacie."

"What?" I whisper back.

"I'm bored."

I smile but shake it away. "It's only been twenty minutes—"

"Exactly, twenty minutes too long."

"Twenty minutes." I hold my finger up. "Since the last time you said that."

He groans and dramatically flops down against the blanket beneath us.

My shoulders shake a little, but I don't look up. I refuse to give into his antics.

"I—" Trent starts as he splays a hand across his chest. "Can't breathe. I think—" He shifts to look back at me with his head laying on his other arm while the rest of his body is all sprawled out on the floor. "I think I need CPR."

"Nice try." I glance back down at my laptop. It's only then I realize how dry my eyes are, and I blink them a few times.

"Fine." He sighs—more theatrics, which will also be the death of me. He sits back up. "How about a cuddle break—doctor's orders."

"*Gah*, no." I flinch away from him. I quickly save my final lap-write up on my laptop before coming face to face with that damn pout of his again. Curse those lips and those eyes and that pout. "Fine." I hold my hand up to shield his smile. "To the break."

"Boo." His shoulders slump again, making me laugh.

"How about…" I close my laptop and slide it next to my backpack before pushing both things higher up on the blanket so I can lay down. "Let's play a game. Two truths and a lie—go."

He chuckles a little as he lays down on the other side of me. "Okay. Let's see." He taps his fingers against his stomach. He lifts his hand slightly, counting with his fingers. "I have a dog. I'm a physical education major—"

"Really?"

He turns his head. "What?"

"That's so easy!"

"You didn't even let me finish."

"Because you made it so obvious. Go again."

"Fine." He laughs. "I have a dog—"

"Trent!"

"Wait, I'm being serious—" even though the vibrations from his chest continue to tell me otherwise. "I have a dog, I'm five foot eight, and I'm afraid of heights."

"*Ooh*, okay." I rub my fingers over the blanket beneath our backs, turning it dark grey, then light grey again. "Mm, I don't know. I mean, you're tall but are you, like, that tall."

Trent emits something between a gasp and a grunt. "I'm not that short."

"I know."

He passes me another glance.

"I swear, I like your height, but I know for sure Zack's taller than you. I think Stephanie may be taller than you, and Savannah's definitely taller than you, too."

"You're really wounding me here."

I laugh. "Fine, fine. The heights thing is the lie. Scared of heights, I mean."

"Yeah."

I roll my head to look over at him. "What are you scared of?"

His eyebrow lifts. "You really want to get philosophical right now?"

I blink back at him for a beat. "*Gah*, no."

He chuckles but flaps his hand out and gently taps my arm. "Your turn."

"Okay, let's see." I look back up at the ceiling. "My middle name is Paige. I hate the color green and—" I drag out the word as my brain blanks. I quickly cover my ears with my hands. "I don't have my ears pierced."

"*Oof*, no fair." He tugs at my elbows.

"Nope! You should know."

"How?" His hands reach for my waist. "You don't let me cuddle you enough."

"Nuh-uh." I sing but then squeak and squirm a little as he tickles my sides. "Guess."

"Fine." He lifts his arm and tucks it behind his head. "The middle name."

"Nope!" I put my hands down just in time for Trent's head to shift and those beautiful eyes of his to land on me, sparkling with curiosity. I lift my hand and graze my finger

along the side of his face. "I love the color green."

He grabs my hand before I can drop it, pressing it to his chest.

"Even though my favorite color is light purple, lavender if I'm being specific."

"And your middle name is Paige." His eyes are back on the ceiling as he hums. "Lacie Paige O'Connor."

"Mmhm." I hum back. "What's yours?"

"I'll give you a multiple choice." He releases my hand as his fingers go up again. "Anthony, Daniel, Morgan, or Liam."

"Interesting. Trent..." My shoulders jump up to my ears. "Liam?"

"Close. Morgan."

"Really?"

"Yeah. I know it's weird."

"It's not weird." I pretend to write it out on the ceiling. "Trent Morgan Montgomery." I let it settle in for an extra second before lightly whacking his chest. "That's not close."

He chuckles. "No, but it is, sort of. Liam is my dad's name."

"Oh."

"Yeah."

I roll on my side. "What's he like?"

Trent looks a little reluctant before he follows suit, resting his head on his arm. "I'll give you some truths." His fingers trace the blanket. "He has a beard. He's a construction project manager. He loves anything to do with hockey and baseball. And he wears a lot of plaid."

"Like Zack—the plaid, I mean."

"Yeah." Trent breathes out a laugh. "But it's always red plaid, and it's always the same shirt with paint stains and

holes. My mom yells at him for it."

"That's like my dad and his doggy pajamas."

"You know… I haven't seen him in so long since he's always traveling for projects. He might not even have a beard anymore. He did the last time I saw him, but he goes back and forth. He did when I was little, though."

"So did my dad. A big scratchy black beard that took up the whole bottom half of my face. I don't know how my mom fell for that."

"No beards for you?"

"No, I mean, a shadow's fine and I guess a little scruff, but like, the idea of crumbs and coffee." I cringe as I roll back to face the ceiling.

Trent chuckles. "Coffee beard breath."

"It's a thing."

"Are you sure about that?"

"Positive. Trent Morgan Montgomery."

"Lacie—" He pauses, and I feel his finger gently trace the hair away from my ear. "No-ear-piercing O'Connor."

A shiver runs down my spine, but I shake it away.

"Okay, give me more."

"More?"

"Yes, more truths."

"More truths." He hums before lifting his elbow and leaning his head on his hand. He traces his finger down the little rainbow pinstripe on the arm of my navy-blue sweatshirt. "How about my favorite color's red."

"Truth," I whisper.

"I—" He looks around as if to make sure no one's listening—theatrics—before he leans down again. "Like driving, you know, out on the open road."

I raise my brows but let him continue. His finger also continues to trace along—too subtle to feel through my

clothes, but still entrancing like hypnosis, while his whispered words sound like a lullaby. Sometimes my professor's voices go right over my head, but Trent Morgan Montgomery, I could listen to him all day.

"And…" He slowly drags his finger back up from the edge of my wrist to the crook of my elbow, and up to my shoulder. "My favorite flavor is vanilla."

I flinch. "Liar. Not fair." I go to sit up, but he shakes his head.

"It's not a lie—entirely."

"No, you realize you are messing with the foundation of this entire relationship?"

He raises an eyebrow. "Relationship?"

"Yes, this whole thing is based on cake mix."

"Thing…"

My hands fly up. "Whatever you want to call it."

Trent catches my fingers. "What if I told you, it wasn't."

"What?"

He moves our hands back and forth between our chests as if we were arm wrestling. "This."

"It's not a relationship?"

"No." He laughs. "I mean, it's not solely founded on cake mix. At least not entirely, on my part."

My eyebrows crinkle before I flinch again. "You did not."

"What?"

"You did not!" I sit up.

"Did not what?"

"Purposely throw the cake mix."

"What? No, no, totally not on purpose." He leans back to give me space. "That was all Zack's fault. If he did, then, maybe." He shakes his head. "I don't know, but during my

senior year in high school, there were hundreds of kids—
maybe even thousands." He briefly flings his head back,
and I can't help but think he really should have been the
theater major. "But some days during my free period, or
on days when I was doing things I wasn't supposed to be
doing." His lips tip up. "While I was supposed to be in
class."

My head rolls back. "You were one of those."

"Not all the time. Just sometimes—anyway, I would
walk past the library." Our eyes lock before he looks back
down. A smile dances across his lips. "And I would see this
girl sitting at a table with her ankles crossed and short dirty
blonde hair, always a little wavy and messy. It would get in
her face, and she'd lift her hand up every few minutes to
brush it away or tuck it behind her ears, all the while never
tearing her eyes away from whatever she was working on."

My lips part. "No way...Why didn't you ever—"

"I didn't want to distract you."

I reach my hand up to trace the collar of his t-shirt. "But
I wouldn't have cared."

"I know." He grabs my hand. "I guess I was also too
scared."

"Of what?" I laugh.

He shakes his head. "I don't know."

"I guess I don't blame you. It's easy to build someone
up in your head, sometimes it's even more fun, but I
wonder..."

His fingers feel warm against my skin as he folds them
around my palm. His hands are as warm as the high school
library on a cold winter day, with the heat cranked all the
way up and a scratchy black carpet lining the floors. Each
square wooden table felt like a little bubble against the rest
of the school. The same way school often felt like a little

bubble against the rest of the world.

"I wonder what it would have been like." I continue as my mind travels back. "What you would have said."

He smiles. "I thought about it a lot. I told myself to ask about what music you were listening to when you had your earbuds in, or if I could catch what homework you were doing, or maybe I would just do the dumb thing and drop something near you, but I always psyched myself out."
I'm torn between a shrug and sigh. I end up doing both. "I guess everything happens for a reason."

"Yeah, but...you really wouldn't have blown me off?"

"Of course not. I mean, I can't say I wouldn't have been confused at first, but—" I stare up at the ceiling, picturing my sixteen-year-old self, who I was not that long ago, and yet right now, it feels like forever. I see her studying and studying and yet still sometimes wishing someone would come over and snap her out of it. "I would have smiled so big."

Trent grins.

"Okay, maybe not so big." I laugh. "But I totally would have smiled."

"And I would have made a fool out of myself from just seeing your smile."

"Okay, Romeo." I reach out and shove him a little. "Red velvet is still your favorite."

"Yeah, but I think vanilla is starting to be."

Our eyes lock again as Trent drags his finger back up my arm. I wonder what would have happened if I looked up back then. Probably nothing, and yet I can't help but think about *everything*.

Someone to sit with when you're alone at lunch, and the cafeteria feels so big, and you feel so small. Someone to scare you at your locker but make you laugh more than

annoyed. Someone to laugh with on an ice cream or movie date, where they'll slide their foot up against yours, and you would know for sure it was on purpose. Or maybe even, like right now, someone to absorb the silence with, just the way he is, sitting beside me, picking up my hand and playing with my fingers as if it's the most natural thing in the world.

"All right." Trent straightens up. "Enough of this."

I go to sit up, but he curls his arms under my neck and my knees.

"Let's go."

"Wait!" I squeal before he lifts me off the floor. "Not a bench presser, huh?" I curl my arms around his neck.

He grins and shakes his head before dropping me on the side of his bed. He yanks the fuzzy grey blanket up off the ground and wears it like a cape as he attempts to jump over me.

"Trent!" I laugh along with him as his legs collide with mine, and the mattress jolts me up a bit. I pass a glance back at my abandoned backpack on the floor.

"Don't look." Trent covers my face with the blanket.

"But—" I push the blanket down. "When was the last time you even cleaned your floor?"

"Nope. You're not getting out of this."

"But—"

"Too late." The chuckles vibrate from his chest as he curls me into his side.

My head falls against him as his hands rub up against my back. The warmth between our chests and the fresh cotton scent from his shirt lulls my eyes to close, but I keep them open.

"You know this is why I wasn't kidding before about your height because your heart. It's always right here." I

hear it beating underneath my head and the tips of my fingers. Beating and beating away all warm and gooey and real.

He leans his nose down on top of my head as he holds me tighter. "I think what you're trying to say is that I was right."

My nose scrunches up. "About what?"

"You like to cuddle." I can hear his smile.

"No," I huff. "But you were right. I was cuddling with the wrong people."

"Totally."

The truth is I'd be lying if I said I'd rather be doing anything else.

CHAPTER SIXTEEN: LAUNDRY ROOM CONVERSATIONS

I stare at the clear circular door of the dorm building washing machine and watch as the clothing spins around and around. And...flop. And...flop. And...flop. The clothing topples down from the top more than it loops around.

"I could have done this when we get home," Savannah grumbles.

"No." Stephanie clicks her gum. "I'm not letting your sweaty clothes stink up the back of my car."

Savannah folds her arms as she leans against the dryer. "When was the last time you washed your ratty ass hair?"

Stephanie grasps the bun on top of her head before slapping Savannah's arm. Then, they continue slapping and yelling at each other in Spanish, which always leads to Savannah making fun of Stephanie's Spanglish. Something about growing up with only one Puerto Rican parent instead of two. All the while, Megan and I trade shrugs and smiles like we always do when this happens.

Megan stretches her arm out and waves a sock between them. It's ironically long and white. "Are y'all done yet?"

"Y'all!" Stephanie and Savannah shout back at her. I

echo it on more of a laugh, while Stephanie and Savannah are back to slapping each other, but now it's in mutual amusement. If there's anything they love more than making fun of each other, it's making fun of other people.

Megan's face instantly clicks back into neutral. Her eyes are the only sign of fury as she blinks back at us before she casts her gaze back down on her phone. It's only when the washing machine beeps that Savannah pats Megan's legs. Megan twists her body slightly so Savannah can open the dryer door below her butt.

My butt happens to be on the gross basement floor, but I'm wearing sweatpants and brought a towel to sit on. The towel is more useful under my butt than the notebook I have perched between my legs and stomach. I brought it to make myself feel better about hanging out down here instead of studying.

"How the hell does your butt fit into this?" Stephanie holds a pair of Savannah's shorts up to her legs. "They literally fit my arm." She barely shoves her arm through one of the leg slots before Savannah rips them back and tosses them in her basket. "You don't know what it's like to have boobs." Stephanie continues as she brings her hands up to cup her chest before she glances behind her. "Or an ass."

Savannah smacks Stephanie's butt with a T-shirt, making her gasp and hop up onto the other dryer in the corner.

I lean my head back against the wall behind me but still can't bring myself to read the words in front of me. The dryer continues to churn and rumble under Megan, but the only other sound in the room is when Stephanie blows a bubble with her gum, and it pops.

"What is that?" Stephanie whispers before she hops off

the dryer. "No, seriously," she says as she snatches something dark out of Savannah's basket.

Savannah turns around from the clothing pile she's formed on the washing machine next to her. "That's not mine. I swear." She hisses after Stephanie whispers something in her ear. "It's not."

I look up from where I zoned out on the floor to find a dark cheetah print bra lined with thick black lace dangling off Stephanie's fingers. We trade wide eyes before all our heads turn to the petite brunette still perched on top of the dryer.

"What?" Megan glances up from her phone.

"Care to explain?" Savannah points her finger while Stephanie raises the bra higher up in the air.

I've never seen Megan move so fast, nor have her almond-shaped eyes widened so much.

Savannah gasps. "Megan!"

"What?" She stuffs the bra up her oversized t-shirt.

"First you wear leggings and now..." Stephanie trails off.

Megan shrugs. "What's the big deal?"

"You *never* wear leggings." Stephanie continues. "I feel like I don't even know you."

"*Jeez Louise*, it's just a bra. Like my mama always says." Megan's accent shines through. "You gotta look good to feel good."

"Yeah, but." Stephanie chokes. "Who knew you had an ass under all those mom jeans?"

"Yeah." Savannah wiggles her eyebrows. "What else are you hiding under there, mamacità?"

Megan tilts her chin up at her. "Wouldn't you like to know?"

"I would actually." Savannah steps in closer to her. "There's

a whole lot of lace on that bra, you know?"

"Never pegged you for a lace kind of girl." Megan points her finger up and down. "With all that spandex you usually have to wear, and, hey now, don't look at me like that. You're the one that's usually slapping all the butts."

"Aw, is that why you started wearing leggings? You want me to slap your butt?"

"What? No!"

"Ha!" Savannah rips the bra out from underneath Megan's shirt and presses it up against her chest.

"You know it's been a while since I've been with a guy." Stephanie practically sighs as she hops back up on the dryer.

Savannah snorts. "What like two days?"

"No!" Stephanie huffs and slaps her with a shirt. "Like two weeks." Her shoulders jump up to her ears in a wince.

Savannah grunts as she tries to put Megan's bra on over her sweatshirt. "Anyone's better than Patrick Gemski."

"Hey!" Stephanie throws a shirt, and it lands on Savannah's head. "Not like your first was any better."

Savannah rips the shirt down and smirks. "Which one?"

Stephanie gasps before her voice drops back down to a whisper. "You did not."

Savannah's ponytail jiggles as she nods. "It was so liberating. It was like losing it all over again."

Their voices drop in and out of whispers. I try to read my notes again, but I still catch on to Savannah saying something about guys giving her the right look or girls pulling her close in the right way. For some reason, Trent's smile pops into my head. His lopsided one and his full one. The small ones when the wind outside is blowing his hair around, and the big ones when he's sideways and trying to hold in his laughter during class.

"Megs waiting for the ring," Savannah whispers and swirls her left ring finger in the air.

"You don't have to whisper." Megan doesn't even look up from her phone. "I'm not trying to hide it.

"Are you sure?" Savannah doesn't look up. She's still holding her boobs. "Tell that to the line of guys that follow you around like puppy dogs."

"They do——" Megan leans over and finally snatches her bra back with a huff. "Not!"

"What about you?" Stephanie slingshots one of Savannah's headbands into my lap.

I loop the black cotton material around my fingers and shrug. "I'm waiting until I feel comfortable."

"That's usually all it takes." Savannah puts her finger inside the side of her mouth and lets it go with a pop.

I roll my eyes at all the giggles that follow.

"You know what?" Savannah whirls around and wiggles her eyebrows at me. "You should just let Meg give you her love spell."

"Curse." Megan cuts in. "Love curse. You don't just want them on their knees. You want to grab them by the balls."

We all cackle like witches, but Savannah leans over for the second time to feel Megan's forehead with the back of her hand as if making sure those words came out of her mouth.

****

They started playing holiday music in the student center, and I've got one week left before I can be dancing along to it in the comfort of my own house. I'm trying to focus on my final assignments, but it's hard when all I keep hearing

is, "This exam is worth twenty-five percent of your grade, which was outlined in your syllabus at the beginning of the semester." No matter how many times I inhale the crisp cool air, I still feel myself trudging back to my dorm. I even dug out my brown leather boots in hopes of adding some pep to my step, but instead, all I feel is tired.

"Hey, stranger." Trent salutes me from across the lawn.

I send him a quick wave before stuffing my cold fingers back into my jacket pockets.

"Hey, wait up."

I slow my pace, hearing his footsteps behind me. Both some scraping against the cement and then some leaf crunching as he catches up to me on the grass.

"Is everything okay?" His voice lowers along with his head.

"Yeah, everything's fine." I wave my hand. "I'm just tired." I go to start walking again, but he reaches out for me.

"Are you sure you're okay?"

Stephanie, Savannah, Megan, and even my lab professor, have already asked me the same question. I should take a sharpie and write I'm tired, stressed, and have my period across my forehead.

"I'm fine, really. Don't you have class or something?" I go take a step back, but he closes the distance with a shake of his head.

A ghost of a smile traces his lips as his fingertips graze the back of my hand. "C'mon."

My body is calling for my bed, but my heart is now iron being pulled by Trent's magnet. He doesn't drop my hand until we reach the passenger side of his car. He opens the door for me, and I plop down inside only because I'm now without the warmth of his fingertips.

"Your car smells like…cinnamon," I say once he closes the driver's side door behind him.

"I'll take it." He laughs and buckles himself in.

I do the same only more slowly. "Where are we going?"

He turns the key in the ignition and looks in the mirrors before passing me another glance. "You'll see."

He checks behind him before slowly backing the car out of the parking spot and continues to drive the same way, slowly and even easily. It isn't long before we pull out of campus and onto the main road. The four-lane road is still dark black and wet from last night's rain, making all the white lines stand out.

"This is my favorite," I say, referring to all the red, orange, and yellow leaves lining the sides of the road. Most of them have already fallen from the trees, but a few still hold on.

"Mine too," Trent says. A beat passes before he seems to straighten up in his seat. "But now for the best part."

"What?"

He keeps his eyes on the road while he flicks his hand out and presses the button to roll down the windows. My hair starts whipping around as we're cresting down a slight hill. The sky feels like it's dipping along with us as Trent begins to yell. It's the kind of yell that comes straight from your gut and works its way up your chest until it sounds more like a roar.

"Trent!" I'm laughing.

"C'mon! You know you want to!"

"But—"

"Now's your chance!"

So, I do. I start to scream at the top of my lungs. It starts out muffled in laughter and halfhearted groans before it turns into one I normally would muffle inside a pillow

because it was midnight and my family was asleep, but I felt trapped inside my head. I scream until my throat feels scratchy, and I'm laughing so hard my stomach hurts. I forget how to breathe, but I don't mind because he is sitting right there beside me the whole time. He laughs so hard that he can't stop smiling and has to take one hand off the wheel every few minutes to rub at his cheeks. Even when silence falls over us again, he keeps driving.

Our inhales are in sync when he pulls us back into a parking spot and turns off the car. He turns his head and flashes me with a smile. Everything feels all colorful and airy when I step out of the car. The dark tree bark, the wet bricks, and even the cement beneath our feet. The sky above us is overcast and white, you could draw on it, but it now feels like the brightest shade of blue.

Trent must feel it too, because when he catches up to me at the hood of his car, he sweeps up his arm and grabs my hand again. Our steps are lazy and slow as our hands swing back and forth between us. By the time we reach my building, I still can't bring myself to let go of his fingers.

"Wait a minute." Trent flicks his head to the right. He tugs me along slowly at first before his steps quicken like a little kid sneaking past their parents' room at night.

We're both giggling and breathless by the time we reach the side of the building. Trent sweeps up my other hand before he starts taking steps closer and closer and closer, backing me up against the bricks.

He brings our hands up in the space between us and threads his fingers between mine, one finger at a time. "Thank you."

I can't stop giggling. "For what?"

He shrugs. "For existing."

"No, thank you." I lean up on my tiptoes and slide my

arms over the thick cotton of his navy-blue hoodie.

His hands slide down my back and wrap around my waist. "For what?" He's only breaths away now as I lean my head on his chest.

"For being you."

He closes the remaining distance between us and leans his head on my shoulder, resting his nose on the skin where my shoulder meets my collar bone.

"Mm." He hugs me tighter. "Vanilla."

I don't know how long we stand there breathing each other in. It could be hours, maybe minutes, but probably only for a few seconds, and yet I find myself planting roots right then and there, piercing right through the cement beneath our feet, branches breaking through the bricks behind my head, wanting nothing more than to stay right here for as long as humanly possible.

CHAPTER SEVENTEEN: UNCONTROLLABLE VARIABLE

"This final is going to be brutal. I can feel it."

"I know." I'm smiling, but it's not because I don't agree with Trent. It's because I can't help it.

It's Monday again, but it's not just another Monday. It's the last Monday before break. Next week, at this time, I will be lounging on my couch at home, but right now, the sides of my notebook are filled with smiley faces, some regular and some with their tongues sticking out. The same goes for the review sheet Professor Collins passed out. Trent kept leaning over every few minutes, scribbling one with his pen. Each time he drew one on my page, he seemed to draw one on my face.

"My man!" Someone shouts, making Trent whirl around.

I don't know who he sees, but he instantly takes one big step away from me.

"Oh, uh, sorry." Trent stumbles over his words, but his feet don't stumble as he continues to step back. He doesn't wait for me to reciprocate the distance like he usually does but rather continues to create it.

The other day, he took steps closer and closer.

Today the sky is bright blue underneath cotton ball clouds, completely cartoon and saturated, and yet Trent continues to take big steps away from me, further and further, until I feel as cold and bare as the dark naked bark of the trees shattering the sky. He bumps into people as he goes.

It's like I'm back across the room again—never first chair.

"Have a good break!" His backpack jiggles as he whips around and falls in step with the crowd while I'm practically pushed off the cement pathway and stumbling on to the grass.

The wind whips my hair around like a runaway train rolling by as you stand on the platform to board. You're all alone as the train blares down on its horn and rattles and huffs across the tracks, moving on without you. A few steps ahead before you usually step into the doors, the large yellow bar reads "CAUTION. There's a gap."

He's nowhere in sight, lost among strangers, and I can't help but think, yeah, there is.

CHAPTER EIGHTEEN: WINTER BREAK

The days of winter break roll by faster than the semester ever did. It's almost too easy to forget about the real world when the holidays cast everything in white lights, and I spend way too much time watching other people live on T.V. Then again, there's always the group chat with Stephanie, Savannah, and Megan that makes me feel like I never even left campus.

Y'all can kiss my ass. Megan talks more through text than she does in real life.

Only if it has mistletoe on it. Stephanie never passes up the chance to use a winky face.

While Savannah never passes up on the chance to use the eggplant emoji.

"Can we bake cookies now?" Layla asks. It's the same question she's been asking me since I made the sugar cookie dough last night and placed it in the fridge, and it's the tenth time in the last twenty minutes she's asked since my mom pulled it out of the fridge to soften. We always bring cookies to my grandmas on Christmas Eve, so we always bake them the day before.

"Sure." I stretch to reach for the television remote on the coffee table and click it off before standing up. "But only because your birthday was yesterday."

"That has nothing to do with cookies." Layla charges back into the kitchen on a mission while I stretch.

"It's your present." I laugh.

"No, it isn't," she chirps back.

"Wait for your sister." I hear my mom say.

"She said yes."

"Oh, okay."

My mom's back is facing me as she stirs what smells like potato soup on the stove because it smells like bacon. For a second, I can almost pretend it's August again with the sun shining down on the house and the humidity wrapping its hands around your neck every time you step outside the door. Only the sky is already dark, and the wind is whipping against the window above the sink.

I help Layla dig the cookie cutters out from the highest cabinet, and she spreads them all out on the table. "Candy cane, gingerbread cookie, star, but no snowman. Where is the snowman?"

I shrug. "We must have lost it."

"But what are we going to do? We can't not make snowmen."

"Here." My mom reaches up into the cabinet. "You can use cups."

"But it's not the same!"

"It's either that or nothing."

"Fine." Layla stomps over to one side of the kitchen table.

I spray two trays with cooking spray and give her one before resuming my position on the opposite side.

"What do we got going on in here?" my dad asks, trotting into the kitchen wearing, you guessed it, pajamas. Surprisingly, green plaid ones, even though it's finally 'tis the season for his doggy ones.

It's weird having my parents home at the same time for a full twenty-four hours as opposed to just an hour lull between their alternating shifts. Especially when he steps into the space beside my mom. They trade around coffee mugs and quick kisses. It only takes a few more minutes before he's shuffling back out of the room with most likely a cup of decaf and almond milk, while he left my mom a steaming cup beside the stove with milk and creamer.

He looks over Layla's makeshift workstation for a quick second. "What are those?"

She doesn't even look up. "Snowmen."

I catch my dad's eyes. His eyebrows shoot up to his hairline above the wireframes of his glasses. "Santa won't think so."

"Not funny," I say, even though I'm smiling along with him.

A few minutes later, my mom slides into the seat at the other end of the table right beside mine, sipping on her coffee. It smells like caramel. She watches Layla and me as we both continue to roll out and cut into the dough, but she only stares at me after a while. It's not in the "I-can't-believe-you're-here" kind of way, rather "you're-standing-here-but-something-about-it-feels-different," and "you-look-different-in-the-best-possible-way-and-yet-now-that-you're-here-everything-feels-right."

It even seems like my dad has talked to me more the last few days than he has my entire life, but that's also because I know he shows love in a different way. He'll ask me to watch a movie, and even though we sit on opposite sides of the room, he'll still share a bowl of microwave popcorn with me. Or he'll ask me to run an errand with him, like buying a new lawn mower because ours broke for the third year in a row or the latest and greatest mop for

wooden floors. He has a shopping problem, and if my mom's too busy, he doesn't want to go alone even though he'll never admit it.

"So," my mom says.

I dig the candy cane cookie cutter into the dough before looking back up. "So?"

"So." She waves her hand.

Layla's tongue is poking out of her lips at the other end of the table, which means—

"She's not listening." My mom echoes my thoughts.

"Okay." I dig in another cookie. "So…" I tune into the music and voices coming from whatever my dad's watching on T.V. in the living room. The sirens can only mean he's torturing himself with another medical drama he loves to point out the inaccuracies in.

"Have you spoken to him?" My mom rips the band-aid off.

Ever since Thanksgiving, I knew I had to tell her about Trent at some point, but it's different over the phone when she miles away. Especially now that she has this little smile on her lips. I've been dying to tell her more details in person because I can't tell Stephanie I like how Trent smells like peppermint. She'd think I'm weird, and she'd think I'm even weirder because I like how he loves to cuddle, and I hate it—but don't hate it. My mom would still think I'm weird, but she's my mom. I like when she laughs at me and calls me weird. It feels like a compliment because I am weird, but I'm the weirdest thing she ever created, and she loves me for it.

"Not really."

"Oh, that's okay. He's probably just busy with the holidays and such."

"Yeah."

My mom gulps down more coffee while I feel myself gulping down my salvia because all I can see is the gap between Trent and me the last time I saw him. I tried to wait and see if he would close it since he was the one that created it in the first place, but the other day I finally caved and sent him a text for the sake of my own sanity—to say at least I tried. It went like this.

Hey, Trent! Just wanted to say hi and I hope your break is going well!

Twenty-four hours later.

Hey, yeah, sorry. You too!

"So," my mom coos again. "What's he like?"

"I already told you." I laugh. "He's a junior."

"And?"

"And his favorite color's red."

"Okay, but what's he *like*?"

"He's…nice."

My eyes flick up to see the deadpanned disappointment written all over my mom's face, but it only makes me laugh again. "He is, though, you know. We study together and watch movies sometimes, and that's really—it."

"That's all you're going to give me?"

"Well, yeah, I mean, I don't know."

Now she's the one to laugh. "What's with all the hesitation?"

"What? I—" I finish placing a gingerbread cookie on my tray. "I don't know. I guess I just realized I don't know that much about him. Like, I know a lot, but still."

"That's okay. It's only been what? A few weeks? You still have all the time in the world to get to know each other."

Of course, she says it like that. She likes to use romance novels as a distraction from the traumas and hardship she

endured when she was only a rookie on late-night street calls at three am.

"True."

I glance up to see Layla re-shaping her dough scraps. The blue latex gloves on her hands seem to be keeping her dough from sticking to the table. I lean over the chair to reach for the flour bag. I didn't go with my mom to buy it. If I'm being honest, I've been avoiding going to the grocery store since I arrived home, and if I'm being *really* honest, it only has half to do with the fact that since returning home, I've become a lazy pajama-clad sack of bones.

The flour is heavier than I anticipate since it is brand new. It bends my wrists. My foot trips on the leg of the kitchen chair as I try to catch it, but it slips from my hands and flies forward, spraying Layla and all her perfectly carved out cookies with flour.

She screams.

One time she shattered a glass.

The neighbors no longer call the cops on us. They used to when we were younger.

Thankfully, they know by now. They know better.

"How could you!"

"I'm sorry. I'm so sorry!"

"I hate you! I hate you! I hate you!" Her bright red cheeks are the only thing I can see as I take two stumbling steps back before the table and chairs all go clattering to the floor.

My parents are blurry blobs of color as they rush to her sides.

"Layla, honey!"

"Sweet pea!"

"I'm sorry. I didn't—"

Layla runs out of the room. Her footsteps pound up the

stairs. My mom is hot on her tail.

"Dad."

He passes me a glance over his shoulder, but he's looking past me. His focus is already upstairs. "It's okay, bean." I can see him taking the stairs two at a time from the doorway.

All the cookies make a pile on the floor in front of my feet. The corners of my eyes sting. I let them. I count to five. Then, I blink and blink before wiping my hands on my pants and bending down to pick the table back up.

****

I make my way upstairs once the kitchen is cleaned of any flour and sugar cookies remnants. My fingers graze the banister as I swerve to the right. I bypass my bedroom, heading towards the bathroom. I slowly close the door behind me, ensuring it doesn't even make a click.

"This anxiety won't hurt me, even if it doesn't feel good. This anxiety won't hurt me, even if it doesn't feel good." My mom's whispers trickle into the silence in between Layla's hiccups as she tries to repeat the chant herself.

I curl myself up in the space between the toilet and the bathtub with my back against the tub and my toes tapping on the edge of the grey memory foam carpet between the two. The heat vent on my right makes a few ticks as warm air continues to pour out of it. It feels both comforting and suffocating at the same time.

I start aimlessly scrolling through my phone, and the minutes tick by. I would say like a clock, but the little white clock hanging above the light switch next to the door hasn't worked in years. It's been stuck on six forty-three. I don't know if it's morning or night. I also don't know what

batteries it takes. I do know my dad took them out one day when we were younger because Layla hated the ticking of the little red second's hand. For months, she'd wake up in the middle of the night screaming about a noise none of us could hear. It was that silly little clock, and the only reason my parents didn't throw it away is because it's one of the only things they have left from the original apartment they both shared when they moved in together for the first time. My dad was twenty-nine, and my mom was twenty-six. She was only twenty-three when they met.

That's only five years older than I am right now, yet that feels like a lifetime away. Then again, it was, and for me, it is.

"Do you need anything?" my mom asks.

A few beats pass before I hear Layla answer. "No."

I used to picture eighteen in my head all the time, and now here I am. It feels just like seventeen, but at the same time, it feels different, or maybe I like to think it feels different the same way I now expect twenty-three to eventually feel different.

Trent's name pops up at the top of my screen with a text message. *Hey.*

Just three little letters that make my stomach do a little stop, drop, and roll into my other organs.

Hey. I type back. A few seconds later, another text floats in.

Are you busy?

No, you?

No. First message. *Any chance you want to talk for a little bit?* Second message.

My stomach flips again. I can't decide whether it's the worst timing or perfect timing, but my fingers still type back my reply. *Sure.*

It's only when his name flashes across my screen again, this time turning everything else black, I start to regret my decision. I remember I'm sitting across from a toilet seat. My leg muscles are starting to cramp, and my lower back is starting to hurt. The heat really does feel suffocating—too heavy to breathe in—and yet I slide my finger across the screen before my stomach can complete another high jump. It's probably going to deserve a gold medal by the end of this conversation.

I press the phone up to my ear. "Hello?"

"Hey," Trent whispers.

My thumb finds my upper lip. "Hi."

"Why are you whispering?" he asks.

"Oh—uh—" I sit up straighter while my eyes catch the door. "I don't know." A beat passes as my brain buzzes. "Why are you whispering?"

"Me? Oh, um...I'm actually—Okay, not gonna lie, I'm actually in the bathroom right now," he says.

"Oh." We both seem to be hiding out in our family's bathrooms.

"Not in the bathroom, though, like not going to the bathroom." He emits a few quiet chuckles. "You know what I mean."

"Yeah." I'm still whispering. I can't help it. At first, it was on purpose, but now it feels right.

"Do you want me to leave the light off?" I hear my mom ask Layla. A beat. "Do you want me to shut the door?"

"Not gonna lie." Trent's back in my ear, back with my stomach and another flip-flop. "I don't know what to say."

"That's okay."

He feels so close yet so far away. On the one hand, that's because he is—literally, but it's more than that. I

want to know what his bathroom looks like. If the walls are a stark white, or maybe a grey, blue, or green. Are there towels hanging on the back of the door? Is there a clock hanging somewhere that works or a mirror instead of a cabinet? Is he sitting on the lid of the toilet, or is he like me, with his butt falling numb against the floor?

"Yo!" I flinch when I hear pounding. "Will you quit jerking off in there."

"I'm no—sorry," Trent whispers before his voice grows louder. "I'm not! Sorry," he says again. "They just don't quit." They, as in, Trent's half-brothers.

There's some more pounding, but it sounds further away. Some music clicks on. It sounds like the standing room of a rock concert but reminds me of the pulse of a dorm building basement.

"They're not even playing Christmas music," Trent says, more to himself.

I smile around my thumbnail. "Sounds loud."

"Yeah."

My house feels so silent in comparison—so empty.

"Hold on one sec."

The music gets louder for a few seconds before it's muffled again, and I hear clicking.

"Sorry, my dog was sniffing. I let him in. You don't like the music either, huh? No, you don't, my big boy, no, you don't." I picture the puckered face to match the nasally baby voice, but Trent clears his throat as if he remembers I'm listening. "Sorry."

"You don't need to apologize."

"I know, I know." He sounds like he's smiling before he sighs. "It's so different when they're here. There's no room to even think."

I shift around but still can't bring myself to uncurl my

legs. "I know the feeling."

"Right, it's like they only come around a few times a year and yet, like, when it's just my mom and me, it's so quiet, but I don't know. Don't get me wrong, sometimes it's nice and all, but—" There's a crash. It sounds like pots and pans, but it could also be a chair or something clattering to the ground. Regardless, it makes Trent laugh. "They're crazy."

Sometimes crazy seems better than painstakingly normal. "Seem" is the operative word. I know things are not that simple. It always seems that way on the surface. That's why we create hypotheses.

"He's still in there? Yo!" Bang. Bang. Bang. "I need to ask you something."

"Sorry," Trent says to me before a much louder. "What?"

"Are you done jerking off?" Their laughter is more like sniffing and wheezing, most likely like Trent's bulldog.

"Jackass!" Trent yells back.

"You're the jackass jerking off."

"I'm not. I'm on the damn phone."

"Porn." One of them coughs.

"I'm so sorry," Trent says, even though he's laughing along with them.

"Hurry up!" They pound on the door again.

"You guys are scaring the dog."

"He's in there with you!" one of them says, as the other one says, "that's just wrong."

Trent sighs. "Just a few more minutes."

"That's what she said." One of them snickers, while the other one says, "fine, the keg is awaitin'."

"Sounds like they're having a party," I say.

"You would think."

"A whole keg?"

"Nah." He chuckles again. "It's a pitcher of spiked eggnog. My aunt usually makes it."

"And your mom…" I trail off because I always forget not everyone cares what their mom, or anyone really, thinks.

"She hates the mess for sure, but like I said, sometimes it's nice."

I wonder what she looks like. If Trent inherited his eyes from her or just his dirty blonde hair, or maybe even his height. Maybe he even looks nothing like her and got all his features from his dad, only sans the beard.

"Let's go, you ding-dong!"

"I'm sorry," Trent breathes. "I really didn't think this through."

"It's fine."

"We should try this again." Bang. Bang. Bang. "Before break ends."

"I'd like that."

"Cool. Talk to you later then."

"Sure, uh, bye."

Another crash reverberates on Trent's end, making him laugh. "Bye."

"Merry Christmas." I add while he's still chuckling.

"Merry Christmas, Lacie."

I pull the phone away from my ear as he disconnects the call. I'm left with the quiet ticking of a nonexistent clock. I'd probably hate all the noise at his house, and yet right now, part of me wishes I could be there just to be submerged in something else.

The blank white walls in here, the lavender walls in my room, and the cream-colored cement blocks that make up the walls in my dorm room are all one and the same. I

thought they were different, but no. They're all blurred together.

I'm thinking of a word, a couple of words, actually. *Numb. Lonely. Home.*

Numb-butt, but it's not just my butt. I don't want to admit it because this is my home. This is where I grew up. This is where I feel the safest, and yet here I am crouched in a corner, not wanting to get up.

I was so ready for eighteen, back in the summer when it was warm, college was still this thing I was planning on doing, and Trent was just a cute boy from aisle three, but now I'm not so sure. I don't know what I want. I thought coming home would make me feel better, remind me that I always have a place to crouch down in, yet here I am feeling lonely.

They say, "home is where the heart is," but I don't know where mine is. I seem to have lost it.

At least he called me. That means he was thinking of me, or maybe—just maybe—he feels numb, too— emptiness in the middle of his chest.

What if he only called me because he was lonely? Not because he missed me. I'm always hypothesizing, but what else am I supposed to do?

His favorite color is red. He has two half-brothers who like to drink out of a keg. His dad is rarely around physically, but somehow, he's always still around. He's a sports medicine major who'd rather be teaching something—anything. He likes red velvet cake, but probably for the color more than the taste. He prefers hot chocolate over coffee, and he also doesn't mind a beer.

I know a lot—a lot of little things. I can't complain. I shouldn't complain. I don't want to complain, but I want more, and I suppose it takes time. I'm only eighteen.

He feels so close yet so far. There's still a gap.

But then again, maybe this isn't even about him. Maybe it's me—me hypothesizing about ticking clocks and ticking time bombs and trains that don't even exist.

****

My sister is the reason my heavy eyelids peel open way earlier than I want them to. I can tell it's early morning even though my room is still dark. The two tiny glow-in-the-dark stars on my ceiling burn bright above my bed—one for me and one for her. They've been there as long as we've been here.

"Lacie? Hey, Lacie? Are you going to wake up now?" Layla has always asked the same question, but I know it's never actually a question because I have no choice in the matter.

"Merry Christmas, Lay."

"Yeah, yeah, come on." She shuffles back out of the room, her slipper socks scraping against the carpeted floor as she goes.

I tiptoe down the stairs to find the white lights of our Christmas tree glowing in the darkness of the living room. My dad is sprawled on the couch with a book on his face. Layla goes to tiptoe past him, but he quickly darts his hand out, making her squeal.

"Nice try, munchkin. You have to wait for your mom. She'll be home any minute now."

Until then, my sister and I sit in front of the Christmas tree like we've always done. My sister likes to guess what's in the few gifts lying under it while my brain is still sleepy, catching only the lights.

"Merry Christmas!" mom cheers when she bursts

through the door.

Merry Christmas b*tches! Savannah texts in the group chat a few hours later. She never shies away from a curse word.

Merry Christmas!!! Stephanie loves both exclamation points and emojis.

If Meg says y'all imma laugh. Savannah jokes when it's closer to dinner time, and Megan has yet to respond.

Megan doesn't mention Christmas. All she types back is: *y'all suck*

Suck what? Anything to promote Savannah's dirty mind. I finally exit out of the conversation when she and Stephanie start sending a bunch of eggplant emojis back and forth.

CHAPTER NINETEEN: NEW YEAR'S EVE

I resist the urge to slap my sister after she blows a noisemaker—again. She vowed to blow it three times every hour until the clock strikes midnight.

"Hey, I want that one."

I raise my brows. "They are literally the same thing."

"No, that one has more."

Layla and I have a stare down as the *New Year's Rockin' Eve* countdown to midnight begins on the television. It's faint because my dad is sleeping down the hall, but it still makes me sigh and extend the wine glass in my hand towards her.

"Fine."

She grins and bounces her slipper-socks against the carpet a little in anticipation as we gently swap glasses of sparkling apple cider. Mom is on speaker when there are three seconds left in the year before all three of us whisper-cheer, "Happy New Year!"

My sister and I clink glasses while my mom sends kisses through the telephone. She was left working overtime in exchange for getting Christmas Day off, while my dad did the opposite. It's an on and off trade every year while Layla and I are always left on the couch in our pajamas watching the ball drop. It's our little tradition that involves taking

down the wine glasses once a year before it changes to the next.

Layla ends the call with our mom, and we flop back down against the couch. My phone lights up on the coffee table. I initially think it's the group chat, but my finger slides across the screen, and my feet shuffle into my kitchen when I see Trent is calling.

"Hello?"

"Who's this?" someone asks. It's a male voice, but definitely not Trent's.

"Who's this?" I bite back.

There's some mumbling and rustling before it seems like someone else grabs the phone. "Why is your contact saved as vanilla? Are you really that sweet?" The following laughter should prompt me to hang up, but instead, I remain just as frozen as my toes against the kitchen tile.

"*Ooh! Ooh!* I got one!" a faint voice says before someone clears their throat. "How big are your scoops!"

I flinch, but the laughter ensues.

"If you're vanilla, why don't we mix together and make a hot fudge sundae?"

"Yeah! I can give you my spoon!"

"*Oh!* And maybe we can do some banana splits!"

I dig my fist into my stomach, wanting nothing more than to throw up every sundae I've ever eaten in my entire life while they continue to snort and snicker like pigs.

"What the—" it's faint, but all the noise stops.

The line rustles.

"Lacie?" Trent's voice is shrill. "Sh*t."

The three beeps fill my ear as he ends the call. My sister's noisemaker shrieks in my other ear as a text from the group chat floats in from Savannah.

Happy New Year hoes!

CHAPTER TWENTY: BACK AND FORTH

It feels weird pulling back up to campus. Winter is in full swing. All the trees are bare, and almost everyone is trudging around all bundled up.

My mom drops me off at the same spot. I trudge up to my dorm. There's a buzz in the hallways as people catch up and chat as if we never even left. I enter the room to find it empty except for my and Stephanie's stuff. The first thing I do is use my hand to push on Stephanie's desk chair, making it take a spin. It almost feels nostalgic.

The door handle jiggles.

"Oh, sh*t."

I run over and pull open the door. "Seriously?"

"Yes! There's my b*tch!" Stephanie fist pumps the air before walking past me into the room. "How was your break?"

"What up, blondie?" Savannah nods at me as she follows Stephanie inside.

"Where's Megan?" I ask, checking the hallway.

"Stuck in traffic, I think. At least she was." Savannah kicks off her slippers and hops up onto Stephanie's bed while Stephanie plops in her desk chair.

"She does have the longest drive," Stephanie says before she starts spinning. "How's your boyfriend?" she sing-songs while Savannah and I both share a look and say

the same thing at the same time.

"Boyfriend?"

"Yeah, boyfriend." Stephanie's hand continues to thud against her desk.

Savannah and I continue to stare back at each other before she shrugs and leans back against the wall.

"Hey, guys." There's a soft knock on the door. "Are you in there?"

"Now that's *my* b*tch!" Savannah calls.

Stephanie stops spinning as I head back towards the door.

"Hey." I open the door wider for Megan to step in.

"Hey." She smiles before taking one big step forward.

I've missed the banter Savannah and Stephanie carry around like luggage, but they are dead silent for once.

Megan keeps her shoulders straight even though she stuffs her hands into the front pockets of her cropped puffy coat. Her hair is no longer chin-length but rather all cut-off, like Audrey Hepburn.

"What?" She shrugs. "I've just always wanted to do it, okay?"

For a second, my chest tightens for her as we all blink and blink before Stephanie leaps up. "It looks so good!"

"You're officially cooler than me," Savannah says.

"She's always been cooler than you." Stephanie ushers Megan to her rightful spot at her desk chair.

I remember Megan posting the selfie of her new haircut a couple of weeks ago but seeing it in person confirms that it suits her. I even noticed she added to her Instagram bio. She/Her/They.

The chatter resumes, just like the group chat, as I take my usual place at my desk chair while Stephanie and Savannah hop up onto her bed. I can't help but think they

all look so comfortable sitting there. I'm still blinking against the flat ceiling lights like I blinked back at my Christmas tree. When I was home, I wanted to come back, but now my brain is filled with all these to-do lists, "home is where the heart is," and I thought my heart was here, meanwhile it's lost in transit.

****

It's the second week of classes, but I still haven't seen Trent since I moved back on campus. We no longer have philosophy together, which doesn't help, and I can't stop replaying the last half-assed conversation we had through text earlier this week. I feel like an idiot and an eggplant emoji and so confused.

Hey Trent! Just wanted to say hi now that classes started! I hope you had a good break!

Twenty-four hours later.

Hey! Sorry I've been so M.I.A. Break got crazy. There was a death in the family and a bunch of other stuff. Been stressful not gonna lie but hope you're doing okay!

No worries at all! This semester is already hitting me harder, so I get it! Lol.

A few hours later.

Hey, just wanted to check in since you said you're stressed.

Thank you!!! But I'm okay! Just new classes and still getting used to things you know how it is.

And that was it.

Stephanie has always said that I text like an old person. I should have said, "I'm sorry for your loss."

I don't know why he was asking me if I was okay when I should have asked if he was okay, and I don't want to pry. If he wanted to tell me, he would have over break, right?

He would have texted me if he wanted me to know, and why should I bother him with my silly worries about my new classes, like how one of my new professors intimidates me, but not in a Professor Collins kind of way. I'm also stuck taking a political science course that makes me miss philosophy, but if his break was so hectic, he doesn't need my problems on top of his.

I'm just really confused because I feel like if he wanted to talk to me, he would have, which means he didn't want to talk to me, and he doesn't want to talk to me.

Call me crazy.

Call me stupid.

Call me a stupid crazy girl who is overthinking too much.

It's simple, though.

If he wanted to talk to me, he would have.

I'm not blaming him at all. I'm just at fault because maybe I should have tried harder over break. I should have tried reaching out again.

And maybe I should try again right now. I should text and tell him I'm bad at all this because I never dated in high school. There were a bunch of longing looks from afar, and then if, a big giant IF, I finally worked up the nerve to say something like, "Hey, I think you're cool, maybe we should hang out sometime." I was always blown off, and then I eventually shrugged it off.

With Trent, though, things are different. I thought things were different.

Yet there's that sinking feeling in my gut, like when I was sixteen with all my other crushes that didn't want to talk to me either.

It was easy to shrug them off because as soon as I was flat-out rejected, it was easy to see all their flaws.

Still, I don't want to shrug Trent off.

I can't.

Call me crazy.

Call me stupid.

Call me a stupid crazy girl who needs to stop overthinking and text him.

But I can't.

CHAPTER TWENTY-ONE: BEGIN AGAIN

It's another Friday, and as per usual, I've got the room to myself. Stephanie is with Savannah, who is also probably with Megan, but who knows. I wasn't paying attention before she trotted out the door.

I've got my earbuds in. I'm listening to some serene sounds considered 'study music' and am typing away on my laptop.

Last semester, I had two different professors for BIO 103: General Biology, one for lecture and one for lab. This semester for BIO 104: General Biology II, I have the same professor for both. She's that annoying dichotomy of passionate yet intimidating. Unlike the same four sweater vests and suit ties my lab professor wore last semester, which made him endearing, she wears cute pantsuits and little Mary-Jane heels with a long white lab coat or blazer. I want to impress her because I want to be her, but her attention to detail, her way or the highway teaching style, is frustrating. Since I have her for both classes, she never forgets a thing. She has no problem calling people out when they make a mistake in lab about something she discussed in class. I'm lucky I have yet to fall victim.

Hence, the 'study music.'

I almost don't realize when the vibrations in my ears are

the silent vibrations of my ringtone. If it wasn't for Stephanie still always forgetting her I.D. card, even though she's getting better, or my mom's check-ins through text, my phone would probably be on silent, which makes it more surprising when I see there are two missed calls from Trent, and even a few texts.

Hey.

Hey, you.

I hope you're not ignoring me.

I promise I haven't been trying to ignore you.

I want to show you something.

My phone starts vibrating in my hands this time, and I pull out my earbuds to answer it. "Hello?"

"Hey."

"Hi."

"How are you?"

"I'm…good. How are you?"

"Why are you laughing?"

"Because—I don't know. Why are you laughing?"

"Because you're laughing. I know it's been a while, O'Connor, but…" I can hear his smile. It's like he's sitting across from me. "What are you doing?"

My eyes fall back on my laptop screen.

"I hope I'm not interrupting."

"No," I say, "not at all."

"Cool, look outside."

"What?"

"Look outside."

"Why?"

"Just look out your window."

"Okay, okay." My arm falls across my chest as I hold the phone closer to my ear. "It's dark."

"Yeah, no sh*t." He's laughing again. "Look again."

The sky looks black. It would be if it weren't for the lamps illuminating the pathways and the parking lot. I can see my reflection tinted in the glass. The ceiling lights are saturated yellow, which is why it takes me another minute to notice the little white flurries bending to the will of the wind.

"It's snowing."

"Mmhm. Now, does your door have a cheese sticker on it?"

"A what? No."

"What about a dry erase board?"

"No."

"School flags?"

"Nope."

"Mm, maybe I'm on the wrong floor." All I hear is his breathing and the patter of his steps. He even hums a little, always filling the silence. "I see a light. What about..."

The door handle jiggles.

I run over and swing open the door.

"Hi." Trent breathes.

"Hi."

We both slowly pull the phones from our ears and hang up the static. He's wearing a black hoodie underneath a black coat. The strings are uneven as if to match the way his teeth sink into his lower lip. He rocks back on his heels.

"Okay." He claps his hands. "Let's go." He strides past me. "Coat, shoes." He waves his hands around all the while his body makes one slow circle about the center of the room.

"Where are we going?" I ask while his eyes continue to dance around the left side of the room. He even reaches out and traces a finger along my comforter.

"We're going...to see the snow."

"How did you know?"

It takes him another second to finally turn his head. "Know what?"

"How did you know that's my side?"

"Because." His lips tip up before his thumb juts out. "You're studying."

"Oh, crap." I quickly hit save on my computer, three times actually, Layla would approve, before closing my laptop. "It's just a lab."

"But you do know it's Friday."

"I know, I'm lame."

"Nah, c'mon." He snaps his fingers. "Coat, shoes, hat."

"Hat?"

"Yes, whatever. Let's go."

"Okay." I move around him and grab my boots from under my bed before going back over to my desk chair to grab my coat. "You're so nosy."

Trent drops his hand, closing the spiral notebook he was peeking into. "Am not." I raise my eyebrows as I stuff my arms into my coat, making him raise his hands in mock surrender. "You saw my room."

"Yeah, but…" I zip my coat before snatching the cream-colored knit hat off my desk. I take the time to stuff my phone and student I.D. in my pockets before glancing back up. "I should change."

Trent shakes his head. "You're fine."

"But you're in sweats."

"You're fine. Nobody cares."

"But I'm in pajamas and"—my feet stumble for a second as I try stuffing them inside my boots— "you're laughing at me."

"No, I swear." He holds his hands up again. "It's just…it's finally cold enough for those fuzzy socks."

"My feet are always cold, okay?"

"Yeah, yeah. C'mon." He opens the door back up and gestures for me to walk first. He turns his head as if taking one final look at my stuff before following me out the door. "Let's go." He swings up his arm and grabs my hand, making us speed walk down the hallway. I start laughing, making him laugh, and then we're running.

We run outside the door and down the steps before Trent fades into the night sky. All I see are constellations of white, all warped and billowing in the wind.

We're both still laughing and running but also twirling and skipping, and we're not alone. A few other people are cheering and squealing across the lawn. At the same time, other people trudge on by, almost as if they don't see it.

I tilt my head up towards the sky. The snowflakes cling to my hair and my hat, but the cold sinks into my skin.

Trent grabs my hand and starts swinging me around. There's nothing calculated about it. There's nothing but wind and air and white. There's nothing but panted squeals and laughter. There's nothing but the scraping of our shoes as our feet dance between the wet concrete and the grass.

"Oh sh*t." Trent's foot slips on the patch of snow piling up in the dip between the pathway and the patch of lawn. I grab his jacket sleeve, but then his other leg swings up, and both of us go crashing down onto the grass. "I'm so sorry." He breathes in between fits of laughter.

I can't breathe.

Both of us keep doubling over in silent laughter now directed at the sky. Every time I go to suck in a breath, we lock eyes again and keep laughing. My stomach muscles start to hurt so bad. I finally give in and lay flat. My lungs take over in their search for oxygen. My stomach expands and deflates with every inhale while the blood continues to

pound in my ears. The adrenaline keeps me warm and makes me sweat even though I'm squinting at the sky.

"You okay?"

"Yeah." I finally turn my head. "You?"

Trent inhales a deep breath before letting it out. "Yeah."

The snowflakes pitter-patters against our jackets. They always seem so heavy, but then they melt away.

"How does snow form again?"

"I don't know."

"You don't know?"

"Nope." I laugh. "I mean, the temperature has to drop low enough, but I don't remember. I'm taking Earth Science next semester, though."

"Oh, it's required?"

"…No."

"You're taking it as an elective?"

My shoulders jump up to my ears. "Maybe."

"Are you crazy?"

"Maybe…"

He flings his right arm out and pats around, but when he can't seem to find my hand, he rolls himself up. One second all I see is snow, but the next second, all I see is Trent.

"Hi." He smiles.

"Hi." I smile back.

He leans in closer. I can feel his eyes dancing around my face—my nose, my hat, my lips. I can't help but do the same. All I see is his nose and his lips. Two red noses. Two pink lips. His are almost too light for his face. He leans closer and closer until—

"Your forehead's cold."

His chuckles vibrate off his chest. "So is yours."

My eyes close, and I breathe in the cold air.

I don't know how many minutes pass, but Trent's smirking when I open my eyes back up.

"I know how to warm you up." He sits up and takes my hand even though my fingers are numb. We start running and laughing again until we stop in front of his dorm building.

"Wait," I say. "I'm cold, but I'm also sweaty now and probably." I cringe. "Smelly."

Trent laughs. "I don't care. Hell, so am I." He tips his head before tugging me forward again. Even though our steps echo up the stairs and down the hallway, I feel just as light as the flakes still trickling from the sky outside. Trent goes to slide his I.D. through the door handle but stops and whirls around. "What I'm about to show you is top secret information." He turns his head from side to side as if checking for onlookers. When he turns back to me, I quickly drop my smile to play along. "You have to swear on your life—"

I bite my lip even though my shoulders shake.

He continues to stare me down, keeping up the act.

"You must swear you won't tell a soul what you're about to see."

I pretend to zipper my lips before throwing in a salute. "Yes, sir."

"All right, then." He turns back around and unlocks his door. His normal posture returns as he flattens his arm across the door and lets me walk in first.

"Why, thank you, kind sir." I bow.

He holds a hand over his heart. "Of course, m'lady."

I walk into the center of the room. The door clicks behind me before I feel Trent tugging on the hood of my jacket. He helps me out of it before hanging it on the back of his desk chair. He shrugs off his coat and tosses it on

the chair instead.

My fingers start to tingle as they warm up. I rub them together before they start to burn. Trent seems to do the same, only he blows on his hands twice before going over to his desk drawer.

"Okay, so." He glances over his shoulder. "Ready?"

I step forward with a nod. "Ready?"

He slowly opens his top desk drawer to reveal a pile of instant hot chocolate packets.

I gasp. "You have a secret stash."

"*Ssh.*" He holds a finger up to my lips. "You promised you wouldn't say anything." I hold my hands up in surrender, and he drops his hand. "Especially, not to the boy who loves to turn anything into lasagna. He'll drink them all."

I cross a finger over my heart. "I promise."

"Okay." He smiles and swipes up two packets. He pulls his desk chair to the side to reveal a bent-over desk lamp, packets of instant ramen, reusable coffee cups, and a mini coffee machine.

He plunks down on the floor, and I follow suit. As soon as he plugs in the coffee machine, he seems to switch our giggling back on. We both sit on the floor like misbehaving kids hiding behind the couch with a pair of scissors.

Once our cups are full, we turn to face each other, sitting crossed-legged. Trent looks at me, looks away, and then takes a sip.

I do the same. Look, look away, and sip.

Look, look away, and sip.

Look, look away, and sip.

I'm smiling before I can help it, and Trent's eyes are shining.

"Why are you smiling?" he asks.

"I don't know." I laugh. "Why are you smiling?"

His shoulders shake. "Because you're smiling."

"Okay." I open and close my mouth. "Let's try to stop."

"Okay." He nods and his lips droop.

I pull my lips in.

His face looks all rectangular as he holds all the muscles down. The longer I stare, the more he looks like a Muppet.

My smile breaks as I burst into laughter. Trent falls forward along with me. My shoulders are shaking, and I try hard not to spill my cup.

When our giggles fade, Trent tips his head up and chugs the rest of the contents in his cup. "You finished?" he asks.

"Almost." I gulp down the last bit.

I'm warm and full when I stand back up, and he takes my cup to toss them in the small garbage can beside the door.

My eyes find my coat, now dry of any trace of snow.

"You know." Trent's voice is low. "There's still another way to warm you up."

My eyebrows rise.

"Not cuddling, I swear." He holds his hands up with a laugh. "At least, not entirely." His eyes dart from mine to his bed and back again.

My first hypothesis makes my stomach dip. I remember what he looked like, all shirtless and giggly. I start sweating again for a completely different reason.

Trent goes over and hops up on the edge of his bed like he did that day. He scoots back on his pillows until his back is up against the wall. He looks back up and pats the spot next to him. When I still don't move, he holds his hands up again.

"I won't bite, promise."

My eyes narrow on the outside, but my heart thumps

against my ribcage on the inside—*boom, splat.*

He holds his hand out to me. "Trust me."

My legs move forward on their own accord, and I take his hand. He pulls me up on the bed, but then he also starts tugging me closer.

I say my second hypothesis. "I don't know. I'm not any good at all this."

He reaches up with the other hand. His finger grazes my cheek as he tucks a stray hair behind my ear. "There's no such thing."

"But I've never really done this before," I whisper because it's my controllable variable. The constant in my life that rings the alarm bells in my head.

"That's okay," he whispers back.

"I don't know." I laugh because it's my coping mechanism. I need to fill the silence to ignore the thumping in my chest. "It feels like I'm driving down the highway without any idea what I'm doing or where I'm going."

His lips curve up for a second. "How about this." His hands flatten against my waist before he lifts me onto his lap. Both of my legs curve around the outside of both of his. He circles his hands around my lower back, holding me against him. "This is me putting on your seatbelt."

I stiffen a little the same way a seatbelt would when you stretch too far forward, and it snaps back into place. I feel like it's sitting on my chest. My hands fist the cotton material of Trent's sweatshirt. My knuckles turn white.

"And this," Trent whispers as he puts his hands over mine. He uncurls my fingers and places each of my hands over his shoulders, forcing me to lean in closer. "Is me putting the gear in drive."

He nudges my chin with his nose as he sits up straighter.

He aligns our lips. They bump into each other when we inhale, but he doesn't press them together. Not yet.

Instead, he seems to be testing a theory because he whispers, "you steer."

A smile stretches across my lips as I finally relax into the warmth of his chest. He's like my own personal cup of hot chocolate, except I can feel him all over, not just in the palms of my hands.

"I really like you," I whisper against his lips.

"I like you too." His smile is pressed up against mine before I melt the rest of the way into him, and we both drink the leftover hot chocolate from each other's lips.

CHAPTER TWENTY-TWO: EXPECTATIONS

I feel Savannah eyeing me from across the room. "Did Lacie finally get laid?"

"No!" I sputter while Stephanie cackles.

"Then why the hell are you walking funny."

"I fell the other day…in the snow, and I started running again."

"*Pft*, okay."

"I still have bruises." I start stretching up my shirt sleeve. "On my wrist, my elbow, and I think even my butt."

"*Ooh*, let's see it." She wiggles her eyebrows.

Stephanie throws her arm up and whacks her in the head. "Deja de estúpido!"

"Deja de estúpida!"

"You never wear your hair down." Megan interjects, stepping up into the space on the opposite side of Savannah. "It's so long."

"And ugly," Savannah grunts.

"No," Megan's voice is quiet. Her fingers reach up to smooth the ends behind Savannah's shoulder. "It looks pretty."

Stephanie and I share a look before Stephanie juts her eyebrow pencil in my direction with a smirk. "She did get kissed, though."

My mouth drops. "How the hell did you know?"

"Did she just curse?" Savannah jokingly elbows Megan, but all I hear are alarm bells.

"I didn't." Stephanie's bent back over her mirror as she laughs. She passes me a glance over her shoulder. One side of her eyeliner is done. "But now I sure as hell do. 'Just studying' my ass."

Savannah's laugh comes from deep within her stomach. "Now you gotta tell us."

"Please." Megan's head pops out from behind Savannah's shoulder. Her lips are all puckered up.

My mouth opens and closes while my brain reminds me of Trent all zoomed in and how his hands felt like they were scaring through my clothes and into my skin.

"There's nothing to tell. We kiss sometimes, and it's— nice. That's it. No big deal."

"Why is your face so red then?" Savannah says.

"So, you should come with us," Stephanie says.

My brain flashes me with the text Trent sent me this morning.

You know I've never had a Valentine before.

"It'll be fun!" Stephanie straightens all her rings.

"Not if she's gonna walk like that," Savannah jokes.

I send Savannah a glare.

"Please, come." I hear Megan say as she plops down in the desk chair.

"Yeah," Savannah grunts. "Slap on some jeans and text your boy-toy."

My lips part while Stephanie shakes her head. "You always take everything so seriously."

"Yeah." Savannah picks are her cuticles. "Didn't you ever date in high school?"

Megan's eyes widen.

"What's the big deal?" I throw my hands up, but when I'm met with all their eyes, my voice lowers back down. "You guys seriously make me feel so lame."

Megan pouts. "Lame?"

"Yeah." I sound angrier than I feel, but it's just the adrenaline, lame adrenaline of a stupid crazy overthinking girl.

"You're not lame, blondie."

"Let me guess." I throw in some finger quotes. "Just innocent."

"No."

"I've never really been good at even talking to boys, okay? The only reason he's even talking to me is because he hit me on the head with a stupid box of cake mix—"

"What?" Stephanie asks.

"Then again, he did say he already liked me before that, but even then—"

"It's okay," Megan says.

"And since when is being serious such a bad thing—"

"It's not!"

I'm not the only one that cringes. Stephanie stands straight, closing her lip-gloss, while Megan stops the desk chair halfway through a slow spin.

Savannah closes her smoky eyes and inhales a deep breath. "It's not a bad thing." She runs a hand through her hair, but then her fingers get stuck in the ends. "Dios mío! I'm sorry." She turns to Megan. "I can't do it." She starts smoothing it up in a ponytail, ignoring Megan's protests. "But—" Savannah turns back to me. "You're...fine."

"Fine?" I almost laugh.

Stephanie chuckles a little.

"Yeah, you're fine," Savannah says. "You talk too

much, but—"

"She's right." Stephanie cuts in. "We all have things we wish we did, or…didn't do."

Savannah coughs. "Patrick Gemski."

"You're done." Megan gets up and starts pushing Savannah towards the door. "Bye, Lacie!"

"See ya, blondie!"

"Are you sure you don't want to come with us?" Stephanie's voice is soft. Her eyes don't leave me even as she throws on her light pink puffer coat.

"No, it's okay. My head kind of hurts."

"I thought it was your butt." I hear Savannah snort from the doorway.

"You sure?" Stephanie asks.

I nod again.

"Positive?" Her eyebrow is curved up over the hope glittering in her eyes.

I turn back around in my desk chair. "Positive."

She catches the door. Megan waves even though I only see her hand. Stephanie smiles and sticks her tongue out. Savannah shoves her head back into the doorframe to wink.

I can hear some of their chatter and laughter even after the door closes, but it fades. I should go back to reading something—anything productive. Instead, I find myself standing up from my desk chair and plopping down in Stephanie's. I use my feet to inch it back to the center of the room before pushing back and spinning. I spin and spin and spin until all the colors in the room converge, and my head hurts.

I know I'm not lame. I'm only eighteen.

Sixteen was lame. Sixteen-year-old Lacie thought

romantic relationships would be fun. Sixteen-year-old Lacie sucked at eye contact and had a terrible habit of always ducking her head, twirling her hair, and biting her nails. She didn't hate Valentine's Day. She didn't make fun of it like all the other girls. She thought when the LGBTQIA+ club sold five-dollar single red roses, it was sweet, and when she saw that another person had actually received one from their person, it was even sweeter. Sixteen-year-old Lacie never even wanted the rose. She just wanted the person that came with it. Sixteen-year-old Lacie was innocent and lame, but eighteen-year-old Lacie still thinks it's such a shame that she never got her rose. Maybe then, when the room finally stops spinning and her eyes land back on the door, she wouldn't be hoping for the door handle to jiggle again.

He would be standing there.

She would open the door.

He would smile.

She would smile.

Maybe he'd even give her a rose, but all eighteen-year-old Lacie wants is for him to say the words.

"Will you be my Valentine?"

But really, all she truly, desperately, naively wants to hear is, "you're mine."

Maybe she should have asked, just texted the words herself. She should have called her boy-toy and asked him out. She could have even bought him a rose someway somehow.

Instead, when it was still sunny out, she replied to his text during the day.

Me either.

When it finally got dark, she waited.

But he never came.
Just like her rose.
Back to reading.
It's all stupid and crazy and lame anyway.
It's only another Monday.

CHAPTER TWENTY-THREE: HALF-ASSED SALUTE

I want to say déjà vu at the first mention of midterms, but I can't because it's not. These are all new classes with all new professors and all-new stress. I know time is passing because almost all the snow has melted, but the idea of studying in a couple of days is enough to make me squirm.

The incessant buzz in the student center is also making me squirm. I don't know what's louder—the music or the chatter. Both keep my head ping-ponging between all the other people in line for Starbucks.

Someone slaps my butt, but I don't even flinch. I glance over my shoulder. Savannah's adorned in her practice clothes and an all too cheeky grin that reminds me of Layla. She slurps on her black cold brew while she waits for me to receive my iced chai before we meet back up with Megan and Stephanie to order food.

Once we all have our trays filled, we search for a place to sit together. I keep a death grip around my tray as I get bumped in the shoulder a few times and skirt around chairs.

"Sorry," a guy mumbles after pushing his chair out on Stephanie's leg.

"No worries," she chirps before turning her head over to me. "I love this game," she grumbles before kicking the leg of his chair as she passes.

Her mass of curls moves out of my line of vision and is replaced by the group of guys all crowded around the rectangular table. There must be four or five conversations going on between them as they choke down their food. I stop in my tracks because Trent is sitting on the opposite end of the table than the guy that bumped Stephanie. He and his red sweatshirt are slouched in his seat as he twirls his sweatshirt strings and nods along to the conversation. That's the same nod he pulled in philosophy class. It's his pretending to listen posture.

His eyes flicker up to mine, and I lift my hand in a quick wave. A smile breaks out across my face, but nothing breaks out across his dull countenance. His eyes remain on my chin as he lifts his forearm up and half-heartedly throws me a peace sign.

The other day, up in his dorm room, the corner of his eyes crinkled with laughter.

"Show me."

"No!" I laughed.

"Please." He pulled a pout. "I showed you."

"Curling your tongue is not a hidden talent."

His shoulders stopped shaking in silent laughter long enough for him to mock gasp. "Is too."

"I need to focus."

"I know." He crossed a finger over his heart. "I promise I'll stop."

"Fine." I wiggled around on the grey fuzzy blanket, getting myself into a more comfortable pretzel position. "Ready?" I faced him and his glittering eyes. I clamped my

lips shut and inhaled sharply through my nose, making my spine spring up and my chest expand. It only took another second for both my nostrils to flatten against my nose.

Our laughter returned only this time it bled into hysterics as I folded over into myself while Trent kept slapping his thighs.

"What..." I inhaled after a while. "Are we doing?" I exhaled.

"I don't know." Trent's smile remained even after all the crinkles and creases on his face faded away.

I sat up straight again. "You know, I also had my tonsils taken out when I was seven."

"You were one of those kids?" He mocked before lifting his hand. "Let me see."

I stuck my tongue out as if I were at the doctor, and Trent eyed the inside my throat as if he was one.

"Yup, looks like no tonsils in there."

I wiggled my tongue around before closing my lips. "Why, thank you, Dr. Trent."

His fingers grazed the bottom of my jaw. His gaze lingered on my mouth for an extra beat before his eyes flickered back up.

"You know, I've been thinking," he said, "about gravity."

My eyebrows raised. "Gravity?"

"Yeah." He mirrored my expression while all I thought about was protons bonded to neutrons surrounded by electrons. Gravity makes your feet stick to the ground, but it doesn't make the ground sizzle underneath your feet.

I found myself leaning the slightest bit forward as if he were magnetic. My eyes went from his to his lips and back again. He came closer and closer until I could smell the

powder of his cologne mixed with the peppermint of his Chapstick.

I reached my fingers up to feel the smooth skin beside his eyes, wanting nothing more than to burn his laugh lines into memory before his lips fell on mine. All warm and gooey, the way honey melts into a cup of tea. After a while, it was easy to forget where he ended and where I began. The same way snow melts into the black pavement, and rainwater rushes into the same stream.

The hardwood floor would be way too hard to lay on any other day, but there I was. I mean, after a little while, I couldn't stop wiggling my head, and my shoulder blades kind of hurt, but everything else around me was soft— Trent's lips, his freshly shaven cheeks, his hair sans gel, and his white t-shirt. I couldn't decide whether I preferred to run my hands through the spike in his hair or keep my own personal fistful of his shirt.

I sat up a little and cracked my eyes open to make sure our backpacks and books were still sitting there on the floor, abandoned like our homework. I guess it assured me that I was awake, and it was real.

"We should stop." I managed to say in between kisses.

"Yeah, we should." Trent agreed but only continued to nudge his mouth against mine.

It all felt like a dream. Too good to be true, too good to stop, until Trent's hands slid a little lower. I was fine with the ways he mimicked me, taking fistfuls of my tank top and cardigan. What made my head fall back a little too hard against the floor was the way both his hands cupped the sides of my hips. His fingers weaved into my belt loops and settled over the hem of my jeans, searing my skin.

"We really should stop." I sat up, pulled at my tank top,

and fixed my hair. I didn't even need to look up to know Trent was confused. His frozen state was a dead giveaway.

"Lacie." He reached out to me, but I drew back.

Legs, move, backpack, phone. I wanted to start working on that jumbled-up list, but I barely moved an inch before Trent grabbed my hand.

"Hey," he whispered.

I froze, but all I could see were the wrinkles I made on his t-shirt.

"I would never." He started, but then he placed my hand on his chest. The same way he did when he was drunk, only this time, he squeezed my hand as he held it there. "I would never force you to do anything."

Now he's using that same hand to throw me another gesture. A gesture that leaves me just as frozen but cold and hollow as opposed to warm and mushy. I don't know how or when my feet start moving again.

"I thought he was, like, your boyfriend?"

I don't know who asks, but my mouth still opens. "No, it's not like—he's not like—"

"Like!"

I flinch as we finally plunk down at a table.

"Still," Savannah says. "That was barely a peace sign. It was like a salute, but a half-assed one."

"Maybe he's busy." Megan shrugs as she pokes at her salad with a fork.

Savannah's head whips around. "That's the best philosophy you got, Meg?"

Megan pierces her with a glare, and the seemingly tough girl's shoulders slump.

"Sorry, I'm sorry." Savannah rubs at her temples for a quick second before pulling half of her wrap out of the

plastic container in front of her. "I'm tired, sweaty, and"— she takes a big bite— "hangry."

"Is that why you're still wearing your knee pads?" Stephanie asks but only gets a nice shove to her shoulder in response. Stephanie's the one pointing and laughing, though when lettuce ends up falling out of Savannah's mouth.

I have a similar wrap sitting in front of me, but I can't bring myself to open it yet. I run my finger over the condensation on the outside of my chai cup instead. My phone vibrates in my bag, and I pull it out to read the text.

Let me guess... you have vanilla tea in that cup.

"Is that him?" Stephanie leans over.

"Yeah." I shrug and opt for the shrugging emoji in response to Trent's text.

Savannah's back to teasing Megan, but since they share a room, Megan easily matches the verbal blows without even batting an eye.

A few minutes later, Savannah's hands flatten against the table. "Does anyone want to go for a run?"

All our eyebrows rise, but Stephanie speaks around the food in her mouth. "I thought you were tired from volleyball practice."

"You mean slapping people's butts," Megan mumbles.

"I was," Savannah says, "but I can't concentrate when I'm feeling bitter, and as for you." She points at Megan. "It's called good sportsmanship."

Megan smirks. "Is it, though?"

"I'll go," I say, pushing back my tray. I've been itching to run since the second we got here, but Trent just gave me the perfect excuse.

"All right, blondie." Savannah reaches over the table to

high-five me.

An hour later, my flashlight ends up guiding the way.

Megan and Stephanie create a makeshift finish line to an agreed race finish. Savannah not only ends up beating my ass, but she also slaps my ass when she passes me. She cackles the last few sprints over to Stephanie while I have to stop and breathe in the night air. No matter how much air my lungs gulp down, my laughter remains. It's that perfect stomach clenching, cheek hurting, silent kind of laughter. My worries about a certain green-eyed boy cease to exist until I wake up the next morning and, once again, replay the way my hand waved, and his only half-assed saluted.

CHAPTER TWENTY-FOUR: MOTION SENSORS

A few days go by before Trent asks me to meet him in the library basement. I've only been down here a handful of other times. Once, Stephanie wanted to use the whiteboard to practice her presentation to me. Another time with Megan when there was some major private family drama between Stephanie and Savannah, a.k.a Rodriguez versus Rivera. I came down by myself a few times when I needed some other blank cement walls to stare at outside my dorm room.

The basement is composed of a bunch of rooms. Each staircase takes you to a different entryway. Some rooms are mini-conference rooms with long dark wooden tables with rolling chairs and windows on all sides for classes or clubs. Some have long tables, chairs, and white dry erase boards for people to do homework and have study sessions. There are even couches sprawled around so some people take the opportunity to throw their hoods up and take naps on in between classes.

All the rooms overlap and look into each other like a continuous maze. Similar to a completely comical chase sequence in movies that's all sped up with silly cartoon

music. People dash from room to room with doors opening and shutting. They always almost catch each other, even taking a beat to make eye contact, but never actually get close.

"Hey," Trent whispers, making me jump a little, halfway through a text asking where he is. "Here." He holds out a cardboard hot cup.

I gladly wrap my fingers around it, embracing the warmth of it against the slight chill in the air. I bring it up to my nose a little and get the slightest whiff of chocolate.

"Thank you."

"You're welcome. Come on." He flicks his head towards the main hallway that connects all the rooms, lined with peach linoleum flooring and two bathrooms on either end.

"Where are we going?"

"I wanted to talk to you about something...about an idea I had."

"Okay."

"Here." He pokes his head into one of the rooms but seeing a few people sitting inside, he keeps on walking, but more like swaying his feet from side to side as if his head's weighing on him a little extra today. He pokes his head into another room, checking for people before waving me inside after him.

My eyes dart between the few rows of long white tables on the left half of the room and the long plum couches on the right. I look over my shoulder, but Trent waves his hand again.

"Wherever."

"Okay." I repeat because I don't know what else to say.

"Sorry, it's—" He pauses as two girls move around us,

chatting and taking seats on the end of one of the tables. "Dang," he whispers. "Come on." He nods back out the door, and I reluctantly follow suit.

He goes directly across the hall and pokes his head into a similar room only with a mirrored set up. Some of the ceiling lights are flicked off, leaving one half of the room slightly shadowed while the other is still haloed in yellow-white lights.

"Here." Trent places his cup on the end of one of the tables and pulls out one of the grey plastic chairs. He yanks it back behind him before pulling back the adjacent chair and gestures for me to sit in it.

I comply, crossing my ankles and keeping my hands tucked around my cup. I wonder if it's warm enough to drink yet and go to take a tentative sip while Trent flips his chair around and sits on it backward, facing me.

"So, there's something I wanted to tell you, something I've been considering."

I take another delicious sip of hot chocolate since I discovered it has reached the perfect temperature where you're tempted to chug the whole thing right then and there, but you don't because you also want to savor every moment of it.

"Okay." I finally nod.

"And I want you to be honest."

My cup hesitates halfway to my lips, making Trent throw his hands out.

"It's nothing crazy, though, I promise. It's not even that big of a deal, really."

I eye the doorway at the sound of people. I see a few pairs of people trickle by before one pair makes its way into the room. The guy's silver chain on his jeans clinks around

as he walks in with, who I assume is his girlfriend, who's wearing a cream-colored baseball cap and sipping on some coffee.

"Dammit," Trent whispers before standing back up and scratching the legs of his chair against the floor.

"Hey," I say. "What's going on?"

Trent scrubs a hand down his face. "Nothing."

I purposely scrape my chair against the floor, making it screech loud enough for the couple to send me wary looks. "Look, I have a lot of reading I need to do."

"I know, I know. But—"

Warmth wraps around my hand again, but this time it's not from my hot chocolate rather Trent's hand around mine. It defrosts whatever ice built up around my frustrated resolve.

His thumb rubs the skin on the back of my hand. "I just want to be alone, that's all."

My steps feel light as I follow him out the door. Each of us has hot chocolate in one hand and holds hands with the other. I want to be mad at myself for getting swept back up so easily, but I picture myself more like a pile of confetti rather than a pile of dust, already shiny and sparkly on my own, while Trent is the broom. He sweeps me up every once and a while just to watch me float around and back to the ground.

He checks into the last room at the end of the hall on the left. It's one of the conference rooms with big black chairs. Only the lights are off. Trent leans back and lets me step inside first, making the lights flick on from the motion sensors.

"Hey, Trent!"

Trent flinches and drops my hand as if it's on fire.

"Wanna go grab some grub with us?"

I go to lean back and see who it is, but Trent leans further into the door frame, preventing me from peeking out.

"Maybe later." Trent waves his hand.

I duck my head to prevent myself from getting a mouthful of his thin maroon sweater.

"*Ah*." The guy seems to drag out the word. "I see. Have fun!"

I take another full step back and catch the end of Trent's grin. He quickly drops it as soon as we lock eyes.

I don't drop my glare. "Really?"

"Just ignore him. That's what I do." Trent walks around me and tugs at a chair.

I feel myself getting cold again, but Trent looks up, and my legs move on their own accord. Trent seems to mess around with the chair a little bit, adjusting the height and swaying back and forth on the wheels. I perch myself on the edge and tap my nails against my hot chocolate cup.

I almost want to say I'm done for today. I suddenly feel like I went through a funny movie room chase, and it weighs on my shoulders.

"Okay, so." Trent rubs his hands together before inching his chair closer to mine. He nudges my legs with his, spinning me to face him. "I've been thinking." He inches forward again, keeping our legs and knees resting between each other's. "What do you think about…"

I start to warm up again as my mind whirls with everything he could possibly say, everything he's been trying to say, everything he maybe wants to say, and suddenly confetti flutters around in my stomach again. While my mind is automatically conjuring up a yes. I don't

know why. Why, why, why is my brain doing that? I don't know. But why, why, why else would he want to talk alone unless it was something about us, maybe, possibly. Suddenly I realize how I've been maybe, possibly wanting something more, a simple yes or no question. It dawns on me. Maybe it's finally happening. Will you be my—

Trent reaches up and grabs his neck. "I was thinking about..."

I inhale as his knee brushes against mine once more.

"Changing my major."

"What?"

Trent leans back a little sheepish. "To a full education major or something."

"Oh." It's not even about us, or we, or me.

"I shouldn't, right? It's stupid?"

"What? No." I desperately try to reign my disappointment back in. I take a sip of my hot chocolate, but it's no longer satisfying. It's cold. "I think...I think it's a great idea."

Trent perks back up. "Really? You mean it?"

"Yeah, I mean, if that's what you truly want."

"Yeah, I think I do." He traces his finger down the side of his cup. "I mean, my mom's a teacher, and I've always admired her for that, but you know, my dad, he may not be around much, but when he is, he certainly has a lot to say." He scratches at his jaw. "I don't know. I guess I did the dumb thing and listened to him in the first place."

"You're not dumb."

"Yeah, but it's hard, you know, all the voices and whatnot."

My head already has enough voices. Stupid, little, hopeless voices that romanticize things like hot chocolate and being alone in library basements and how vanilla and

red velvet don't traditionally go together, but we do. I thought we did. I thought we have been.

"It's the thing, you know, the whole 'teaching isn't truly manly' and all that prehistoric sh*t. Even Zack being a theater major, pushed his buttons but only a little less because—"

I echo the end of Trent's sentence word for word. "He can make a lot of money."

"Yes." He breathes. "Exactly. I knew you'd get it." He passes me a glance as he picks up his hot chocolate and finally takes a sip. He flinches. "*Oof*, it's a little cold." He takes another sip anyway before shaking his head. "Anyway, thanks for listening. I feel like you're the only one I can really talk to about this stuff." He stands back up, taking all the warm air in the room with him. "I'll leave you alone now so you can do some homework." He takes another sip of his hot chocolate as he takes another step towards the doorway. He already feels miles away. "Dang, we seriously waited too long."

"Yeah..."

I did.

CHAPTER TWENTY-FIVE: REALLY NOTHING

Come cuddle with me.

The words blink back at me for a few seconds before my cell phone screen turns black. A minute rolls by, and my screen lights up again, reminding me of the text. The answer should be simple. Yes, no, maybe so. My stomach tightens at the thought of saying anything at all. I could keep reading and pretend I didn't see it, but I did that the other night, and over the weekend, my excuse was, "Sorry, I fell asleep."

My phone screen goes black again while maybe blinks around in my mind. Maybe, maybe, maybe. Maybe I've been reading this all wrong.

I tug at my lip. The reading I was in the middle of now completely abandoned. My eyes are glued to the end of my comforter. It doesn't help when my phone lights up again.

Correction: come study with me? Trent tries again.

I finally pick my phone up off the desk. *Library?* I ask because even though the study sessions in his dorm room are never really productive, I might as well drag him down to the basement for another real talk. It feels necessary at this point, even if I don't want to go through with it. I can't let the nagging feeling I've had in my gut since the other day go. The way he dropped my hand. The half-assed

salute. Two steps forward, and yet always one step back.

I go back to highlighting the article I'm reading at my desk for a few minutes before my phone lights up again. *NoOoOoOo.*

My lips tip up. I can't help it because that's the Trent I know, that's the Trent I've been getting to know these last few months. It's only every once and a while he flips a switch and leaves me in the dark.

My thumbs hover over the screen. Yes, no, maybe so. *Fine.*

He sends me a smiley face in response. The same smiley face I picture his face stretching into. *Text me when you're on your way.* He adds as a separate message.

I send him a thumbs up before placing my phone back down. I stretch my arms up before grabbing my highlighter. I might as well finish what I can before I leave.

****

My purple rainboots squish into the grass as raindrops continue to pelt against my head. I'm wearing my black windbreaker with the hood not only pulled up but also the strings pulled, so the sides are taut around my head. The hitchhiker look is completed by my backpack flopping behind me.

Trent's not waiting outside, or near the door. He usually springs it back with the gallantry of a knight and ushers me inside, or sometimes if he's feeling extra goofy, he'll crack it open, poke his head from side to side to make sure we're clear from followers like spies before letting me in. Most times, my favorite times, are when he waits outside the building or right by the door. He'll perk up when he sees me, open the door with a lazy smile, and then before the

door even closes behind us, he'll momentarily tug me into his side for a few steps, hugging me against him.

"So, how are we today?" He'll grin down at me.

"Not bad. How about yourself?" I'd smile back.

Today, he's nowhere in sight. I'm stuck waiting, but I don't mind because it gives me more time to muster up the courage to talk to him, like really talk to him, no jokes, no pit stops, no detours. My hands wring together at the thought.

Two girls notice me as they walk past me to get to the door and thankfully hold it open for me. I'm glad the hood didn't scare them off.

I clomp my way up the stairs, peeling my hood off as I go, and attempt to fix my hair. I'm a few steps away from throwing it up in a ponytail.

Can I ask you something—no, we need to talk about something—no, look, this is random but—no, look, I understand if you don't want to use labels, but I need—

I lift my hand up, make sure it's two hundred and twenty-seven, before knocking. I quickly retract my hand and wait.

I understand if you don't want to use labels—it's totally fine with me—but I just need—

I lean in closer to the door at the sound of laughter. I lift my hand and knock again. The laughter and chatter continue, so I lift my hand and knock harder, only to wince at myself and curl my hands back.

I understand if you don't want to use labels, but I need to know if—

"Whazzz up?" Zack's head finally pops up in the crack in the door. He throws it back the rest of the way, and I'm greeted by a bunch of eyes blinking back at me. They fill both beds, parts of the floor, and the desk chairs—all with

their different skin colors and hair types. I would love to know all their different Punnett squares to see all the different DNA combos. It only makes sense since it's a Monday night. Trent and I usually hang out Tuesdays, Thursdays, Saturdays, and the occasional Friday or Sunday.

"Trent's not here." Zack goes over and leans on his empty desk chair. "He's doing the laundry." He uses quotation marks.

"A.k.a." One of the girls on Trent's bed, wearing a lacey teal leotard, also uses finger quotes. "Having a poker night in the basement."

"Where they"—another girl with curly red hair and round wire-framed glasses throws her hands up— "don't drink."

"And pretend their mafia bosses." A girl on the floor grunts, not bothering with the quotation marks but rather pushes at the curly bangs on her head. They immediately spring back.

The guy sitting at Trent's desk chuckles as he continues to type something into his laptop on his desk. The blue hue from the screen reflects off his chocolate skin. "You guys are making it sound so scary." He looks up at me. "Don't be intimated by them—or us."

"Or do." The other guy sitting on Zack's bed pipes up, his voice the deepest note on a baritone. "We are pretty cool."

"Yeah." Zack laughs. "Feel free to hang with us instead. That there is cowbell." He points to the girl in the leotard. "Medusa." The girl with the dark hair. "Dane. Fischer." He points to the two girls on the floor. "Sammy." The redhead. "Metal." The boy on his bed throws me a tip of his hand. "And Hi-C." The guy sitting in the chair promptly gives me a little prayer bow.

"Are you done?" The girl in the leotard arches her brow.

"Yes, take it away, captain." Zack salutes her before flopping down in his seat.

The girl scoots up a little on the bed. "I'm Bellamy."

The girl beside her can't stop laughing. "We're actually doing this? Okay, yeah, Melissa." Her curls are brown and red and spring up every which way on her head.

"Claire." The first girl on the floor chirps, while the other girl sends Zack a look.

"Carrie."

"Sam." The red-headed girl lifts her hand. "Yeah, it's not that different."

"Mine either." The guy across from her on Zack's bed chuckles and lifts his hand again. "Steele."

My eyes fall on the guy sitting at Trent's desk, who sighs good-naturedly. "K.C."

"Oh!" Zack springs up again, like the human yoyo he is. "I almost forgot." He goes behind me and grabs my shoulders. "This is peas."

Bellamy laughs. "I thought cowbell was bad."

I tug at my backpack straps. "It's a long story."

"It's not that long." Zack chirps.

"Lacie." I wave my hand in a circle with a smile before looking back at Zack. "I better go find Trent."

"Sounds good. Remind him to give me back my chips."

"The Star Wars ones?" Steele asks.

"Hell no. My potato chips. He brought them down with him, and I want them back."

I shake my head and start backing towards the door.

"Oh, hey, if you happen to see my boyfriend, Henry." Carrie pipes up from the floor, finally looking away from her laptop. "Tell him I'm still waiting for my coffee."

"Will do." I laugh a little now, knowing her general

annoyance is with him.

Zack flops back down in his desk chair and picks up a paper. "Can I be Løvborg this time?"

"You're not cool enough to be Løvborg."

All their laughter trickles behind me as I finally close the door.

I rub at my raindrop-stained leggings as I clomp back down the hallway. It takes a few steps for my brain to jump back into business.

Hey, can we talk? It's nothing serious, well, actually, it sort of is kind of serious, it's just—I'm not trying to make a big deal or anything, but I just wanted to know—no, I need to know—we don't have to use labels if you don't want to, but it's been a while, you know, so I just wanted to know if—

Each step down the stairs feels like another weight on my shoulders. My boots echo through the silence usually swallowed by basement party chaos. If there was music, I also probably wouldn't hear any of the laughter.

"No, seriously, spill it."

"How 'bout a drum roll?"

I stop in front of the basement doors as a bunch of rumbling and hollering bounces off the walls.

"C'mon." The same person drags out the words. "You've been hung up on this girl for months. What's up with that?"

"Nothing," someone grumbles, but they all begin banging their hands against the washing machines and tables again.

I gently press my fingers against the right door and go to push it open.

"What's her name again? Lacie?"

My fingers fall back down as I step back.

"Oh, nah, it's vanilla, remember?"

"Oh, yup! That's it!"

I'm surprised their laughter doesn't crack or shake the foundation. It rattles my bones.

"Now you've got to tell us!" another guy mocks.

"Yeah, how sweet is she?" another guy asks. "I bet she's pretty sweet!"

The apple and pretzels I ate earlier suddenly feel like rocks in my stomach—all sharp, jagged, and heavy.

"Have you at least—you know?"

I gulp as my fingers hover over the door once more.

"Yeah, man! You've at least tapped that by now." ,

"Oh yeah!" The rumbling and laughter start up again, with even some high fives in between.

I check behind me, ready to leave, yet also wanting someone else to hear this.

"Enough!" Trent shouts, and I almost jump into the door. "Look, nothing's going on between us."

"*Psh.*" Someone hisses. "You couldn't have known this girl for months and not have gotten a little, you know, something-something."

"No," Trent says firmly over the snorts and snickers. "It's not like that."

Right, we don't need labels but—

"What is it like then?" another guy coos, but I continue standing there with my knees locked and my pencil case stabbing my lower back.

"It's really nothing, okay?" Trent sighs. "She's some girl. She doesn't mean anything to me."

My lips part, but nothing comes out—not even air. My boots squeak as I stumble back. I throw my hand out against the wall to brace myself, but it's too late. I double over as both my stomach and backpack weigh me down.

"She's just some girl. She doesn't mean anything to me."

There's dirt and grass all over the tops of my boots. The air feels too warm as I breathe it in. My heartbeat gets louder and louder until it covers the words that continue to echo in my head. I feel it pounding away in the tips of my fingers as I squeeze them into a fist.

I dig my fist into my stomach as I stand back up and kick open the basement door. I relish in the way it clatters back against the wall and silences everything else. My steps are slow and deliberate as I come face to face with Trent and his friends.

They're all gathered around the appliances and a rectangular table with playing cards, snacks, and red solo cups. Some are sitting, and some are standing, but all their eyes look like they're going to pop out of their skulls. I almost wish they would.

"Sh*t, Lac—" Trent digs his hand into his hair.

"Huh." I click my tongue as I continue to pace around on my side of the basement. My hands find my hips and a trace of a smile almost finds my lips. Almost. Instead, I lift my head back up. "I didn't mean to interrupt. Please." I gesture with my hands. "Keep going." My face feels hot, but I continue to dart my eyes around. "No one?" I watch as half of them scratch their jaws while the other half's Adam's apples bobble as they swallow.

I'm burning from the inside out, yet I still sense the cold down here compared to the crowd of people with Zack upstairs.

Trent's chair goes flying back as he stands up. "Lacie, listen, it didn't—I didn't—" he stutters. He goes to step towards me but hesitates.

Every step back, every stutter, every distance look, half-hearted wave, and sheepish smile all add up to that hesitation.

"Is Henry here?" I ask. They all blink back at me, so I repeat the question with more force. "Is Henry here?"

"Oh, um, yeah?" A guy with square glasses nervously gulps. I keep my eyes glued to him—anything to avoid the burn of Trent's gaze.

"Carrie wants her coffee."

"I'm dead." He squeaks and wrenches back his chair.

"Busted." Another guy snickers, but the guy sitting next to him is quick to slam a hand in front of his chest to make him stop.

Henry scurries on past me. I take that as my cue to shove my hood back on and twist back around. My clomping fills my ears again, along with my heartbeat, as I run back up the steps and out the door.

"Wait!"

"Weak!" Savannah's voice rings in my ears from a memory of her and her black coffee.

My hood flies off, but the rain does nothing to stop the red-hot fury boiling inside me, nor does it stop the red-hot tears from flooding into my eyes. My rainboots and the ground go in and out of focus. I just keep track of each transition from cement to grass.

I double over again when I reach the side of my dorm building. My backpack falls onto the ground, and my wet hair flies into my face. I clench and unclench my fists and bite my lip, willing the tears not to fall, but they do. The adrenaline seeps out of me as I slowly slide down against the bricks and curl up into a ball.

CHAPTER TWENTY-SIX: STUPID MEANINGLESS THINGS

The sky is still grey, the rain has stopped, and my throat is dry.

My legs wobble a little as I stand up, but I still manage to wipe at my cheeks and grab my backpack. I allow my legs to carry me forward into the building all the while thinking about water and the bathroom. My water bottle and the toilet. The toilet and the sink. The toilet, the sink, and the shower.

"*Ay*! Look who it is!" Stephanie's greetings usually make me smile, but I don't even look up.

"Red face, messy hair—" Savannah begins slapping Stephanie's arm repeatedly. "They totally did it."

"No way!" Stephanie bellows before they both begin shoving and smacking each other on the bed. Their bickering fills the silence like it always does while I gather up my toiletries.

Megan slowly swivels around in Stephanie's desk chair. I can feel her eyes on me in my peripheral vision, but I still don't look up—sweatpants, flip flops, face wash. I continue the checklist as I continue piling clothes on top of my shower bag.

It's only when I can hear my rainboots clomping against the floor again that I realize silence has taken over the room. I focus on assessing my pile: towel, hair towel, extra towel.

If only Stephanie and Savannah would start bickering again. If only I remembered to shut my phone off.

The buzzing is persistent. It probably hasn't stopped since I walked in.

If only I were the only one listening.

I stomp my way over to my backpack and quickly hold down my phone's power button before I can read just how many missed calls and texts. I whirl back around, and my head lifts for the first time since I walked in.

Stephanie's shoulders sag. "Red rimmed eyes."

****

"I can't believe this. No, screw that! I can't believe him!" Stephanie continues to wave her hands around.

Savannah snorts. "The definition of an ass and a hole."

Megan hums in agreement.

I continue to stare up at them as they pace around me. My hair is now wet from my shower, but I don't know about Savannah's. Hers could be wet from the rain, her practice, or her shower after practice even though she's still wearing her headband.

Stephanie's hair is thrown up in a bun that continues to bounce around with her movements. Her pink toenails are poking out of her plaid pajama bottoms, while Savannah and I wear socks.

Megan's tan moccasin slippers continue to scrape against the floor as she completes the carousel of pacing

and ranting above me. I've almost been tempted to start singing carnival music as I lay on the floor. I've even lifted my arms a few times in mock conducting before dropping them back down.

I initially came back from my shower to an empty room—nothing but me and the walls and the chatter down the hall. The laughter echoed every once and a while like firecrackers, and the whispers lingered, swept under the cracks in the doors. I want to say it's because they were all giving me space, but I know better. I know I only have myself to blame.

Stephanie was at her study group. Savannah was at practice. Megan was at some poetry night or club or something. All while I'm lying here. I can't blame them. While everyone else is living their lives, I got myself wrapped up in a boy.

I can't blame myself for that either, even though I want to because eight months ago, the girl standing in the grocery store never would have guessed. I tried not to expect too much from my first year of college, but I know I never expected it to end up like this. I never expected myself to end up like this on the floor of my dorm. Sure, we always dream. There's always a little hope in the back of our minds—even if we don't want to admit it—of what could be—all the possibilities. The potential of faraway glances to turn into so much more. But the expectations never exceed beyond logical reach—that is, they are always far too irrational to be nothing more than daydreams.

The reality is the hardwood underneath my aching shoulder blades. It's my face in the mirror, puffy-eyed and red-rimmed. It's this feeling that after months of daydreaming, I'm finally awake.

"I don't get why he would say that." Stephanie continues as she steps over my legs.

"Because he's an a**hole." Savannah has started doing arm stretches as she walks.

"But after all this time—" Stephanie trails off.

"Like I said, ass—" Savannah flings her hands to one side. "—hole. A**hole." She makes the gesture two more times before dropping her arms.

Megan continues to shake her head, showing her disapproval on the subject before they all stop. Their heads become shadows as they bow over me and shield all the light in the room. Stephanie scrunches her nose, Savannah's eyebrows wrinkle, and Megan's lips form a thin line, but all their hair goes falling forward at awkward angles.

I blink up at them for a few seconds before my shoulder blades dig into the floor as I shrug.

"Seriously?" Savannah asks. "That's all you got?"

No! I want to yell, but instead, my posture slumps back down.

"No!" I yelled one time when Trent tried to draw a smiley face on my textbook. He did it anyway.

"Stop!" I squealed when he started tickling my sides in between kisses, but he didn't. He just kept wiggling his fingers and covering my cheeks with his lips.

"I really like you." Trent's lips brushed up against my ear when we were watching a movie on his bed underneath all his fuzzy blankets.

I've got a lot of things—a lot of stupid, meaningless things.

A few hours ago, I had this whole person.

Now all I have are all these stupid, meaningless things.

****

"You wear a lot of stripes," Stephanie had commented one-day last semester. I didn't believe it until I packed up my trunk, but I only embraced it as the days went on.

Trent doesn't have a similar staple. Him and his sneakers and sweatpants and T-shirts and jeans are everywhere on everyone. It doesn't matter that one of his shoelaces is frayed or that he more often wears a V-neck than a scoop neck. It's all the same when I'm walking across campus.

All it takes is light hair and one of the above items, and my lungs stutter on an inhale or exhale. All it takes is a sneaker to squeak or a couple of guys to laugh, and my stomach detaches itself from my esophagus and goes flapping around against my intestines.

It's never him.

I pray it's not him.

Yet I still hold my breath. I still pass another glance back because ninety-nine percent of me dreads while one percent of me still hopes.

"Who said that was a bad thing?"

"I love when you talk science to me."

"She's just some girl. She doesn't mean anything to me."

I glance up from the cement pathway and identify the most prominent white oak trees on campus. Dogwood trees come in a close second. I know that now because of plant biology. I also know the reason I look up is not to identify the tree but because Trent happens to be standing there, staring back at me.

The earth's axis is tilted twenty-three-point five degrees, there are four chambers in the heart, and it's been

three days since I've seen him. Not just his hair or his shoelace. Or someone who has similar hair or shoelace.

And it only takes him three strides to cover the distance between us. I'm on the cement pathway while he cuts a corner on the grass. He only has a notebook clutched in one hand and thankfully no snickering friends behind him.

"I'm sorry." He blurts out when he reaches me and startles me enough to stop looking for an escape. "I'm...*sorry*." He breathes as if just noticing the rapid up and down movement of his chest.

He's still too saturated. Even when the sun darts behind the clouds, and we're left in a dim shade. His skin looks orange against the white of his shirt, and the lighter strands of his hair could be mistaken for bleach. He scratches red marks into his neck and jaw, but my jaw tightens when he looks up.

He may wear the same sweatpants as everyone else, but no one has his eyes. In every stupid, meaningless thing, in every random recollection, I've blurred them out because they're too vibrant, too bright. They don't belong there. They no longer deserve to be there.

Yet here they are, staring back at me with the same pain I've been wearing in the mirror. But while my irises are draining, fading into the background, his are dripping and burning into the forefront.

"Lacie, I—" he starts. "I know I'm sorry isn't good enough, but I—" He stuffs his hand back into his hair. "I don't know what else to say." He moves his head back in my line of vision when he catches me breaking eye contact. "That's not—what I mean is, nothing else seems good enough."

I find myself only nodding because the one percent that

hoped never expected this. The one percent that hoped has finally transferred all its power over to dread, and my tongue continues to pierce my cheek instead of trying to formulate a proper sentence.

"Look." Trent takes a step forward. "I didn't mean what I said, okay? I mean, you know how guys are."

My spine stiffens. "No, actually." I can practically hear all the gears in my brain clicking back into place. "I don't."

Trent's gaze falls as he reaches for his neck again.

"Because I thought I knew you." I click my tongue. "But apparently, I don't."

The commotion outside seems to have evaporated like the clouds as the sun stretches back out.

The warmth now only feels more like a spotlight as I take a step back. "Then again, I'm just some girl, so what do I know?"

A twig snaps under my foot as I take another step back, and another, and another, before I shrug. I wait until his shoulders finally slump in defeat before I turn around and walk away. It's the first time in days I don't glance back.

CHAPTER TWENTY-SEVEN: BRING TO A BOIL

The weather is finally getting warmer, but this classroom is always cold. I'm always reluctant to pull off my jacket, or I bring an extra sweatshirt. Today, the sunshine leaking through the windows on the opposite side of the room allowed for only a sweatshirt.

My professor's lab coat is tinted blue because of the projector light. She continues to lecture about the loss of biodiversity in plant species.

I keep my backpack pressed against my legs as I continue to take down notes. When it vibrates the first time, I don't think much of it. The second, third, and fourth times are no different because I assume it's Savannah yelling at Stephanie or making fun of Megan in the group chat. It's only when I start to lose count, and the sound even pulls the sleepy people around me upright in their seats, do I finally push my chair back.

Freaking Bullsh*t. Savannah's texts float in from the group chat. *Who the hell does he think he is? And who the hell is that b*tch?* She says a few more explicit things, but Stephanie sends another picture that covers it.

People suck. Savannah continues. She always types fast.

Agreed. Megan finally chimes in.

All the while, Stephanie continues to send pictures. My steps falter in front of the bathroom when I finally click on them. I hoped they had nothing to do with me or the green-eyed boy who shall not be named. "Who-what-when-where-and-why the f*ck" should I care?

There's a bunch of candid photos of a group of guys. Some are making funny faces and jokingly choke, holding each other. Others are just grinning at the camera like fools.

All I see is a smiling green-eyed boy with a red plastic cup in his hand and his arm around another girl. It's probably a coincidence she's there. *She's* just some girl. *She* doesn't mean anything to me.

It's him—he's not just some boy. He's the same boy with the purple-bagged, solemn eyes that held my gaze a few days ago. The same light eyelashes, dark eyebrows, and sunspots, but now with the addition of crinkles in the corners. Crinkles I used to want to trace my fingertips along and instill in my memory. Now all I want to do is pinch them between my fingers until they shrivel up and disappear.

I really hate people. Savannah continues.

Megan goes to type something but stops.

??? Stephanie sends me a separate text message.

I lock my screen, so it goes black, and head back into my classroom feeling colder than when I left.

****

I'm the first one out of the classroom, but each step I take feels heavier and heavier. I clench and unclench my fists,

bite my lip, and blink way too many times. I wish my body would stick to one emotion, but instead, here I am.

Sad because I miss him. Angry at myself for missing him.

Sad because I used to have this whole person. Angry because I shouldn't have let myself get so used to having this person.

Sad because I still care even though I don't want to. Angry because now it seems like he doesn't, and maybe never even did.

Sad because I want to go back in time and pretend like I heard nothing. Angry because what if everything I ever heard was nothing but a lie.

I slam the door closed behind me and throw my backpack into the floor. I kick off my shoes, rip off my sweatshirt, and dig my hands into my hair.

But the corners of my eyes still sting.

No matter how many things I bang, push, and shove open or closed. No matter how many memories I bang, push, and shove away.

Everything continues to boil to the surface.

I dig my phone out of my bag and click on a contact, but then there's a knock at the door. I go over and push down on the handle. I don't even look up as I throw open the door and turn to walk away, but my eyes catch on to plaid. It's not the black and red checkered plaid that Stephanie usually wears, but rather a white, red, blue, and even yellow-lined checkered pattern.

"Zack."

He stuffs his hands in the front pockets of his jeans.

"How'd you even..." I trail off. My thumb is still hovering over my phone.

Zack flicks his thumb over his shoulder. "Cowbell."

"Oh." I didn't even know she lived in this building. Now you can call me crazy, stupid, and oblivious.

"Yeah." He sways a little on his feet.

My eyebrows furrow. "Are you okay?"

He looks up, looks back down at my feet, and then looks up again, almost smiling. It's that ghost of a smile that finally looks the most normal on him. Not the sagged, stiff posture and plain white vans.

"You're really asking me...if I'm the one, that's okay?"

My body stills again. "Let's not do this." I reach for the door.

"No, please." He steps forward. "I know it's not my place—"

"You're right. It's not."

"I know, but Lacie." We lock eyes. His are warm, middle of a sunflower brown, like my sister's. His shoulders sag again as he steps back once more. "I've known the guy for years."

"I know, but—"

"I know." He looks back up at me. "I know he messed up. I know he's not five, and I can't fix it, but I just wanted you to know that he cares about you—a lot. I don't know why he said what he said. I mean, I do, actually. He's got an ego as big and square as his head."

"Yeah." I huff even though my mind pictures that big square head of his. A big ball of tears—no, I'm sick of crying—emotion settles in my throat.

"I know I can't apologize for him, but I—I don't know. I guess I really—I came to check on you, that's all."

One side of my mouth quirks up for a split second.

"Thanks, Zack."

He nods as he takes another step back. We lock eyes again, and he sends me a similar split-second smile that also doesn't reach his eyes.

"You know." He rocks back on his heels once more. "I should have called dibs."

"You what?" My heart jumps into my ears.

He shakes his head. "I'll see you around, okay?"

I go to close the door but find my head poking out into the hallway instead. "You technically did though."

He freezes mid-stride, his left foot leaning forward with his heel still in the air, as he looks over his shoulder.

"You're the one that hit me."

His eyes hit the floor first before flicking back up to mine. "Yeah, but it's not the same." He blinks at the ground one more time before his lips curve up to one side. "Plus, I've still got Stephanie to impress."

My lips curve up once more, bigger this time. "I definitely think you're growing on her."

"Good." He nods, sends me a wave, turns, and ducks his head as he trots back down the hallway.

I close the door and find the room looks different than when I came in a few minutes ago. It's not just because of the few things I threw around, like my comforter and desk chair, rather another wave washes over me—the reverse of the calm before the storm. I was the storm. I've been storming the last few days, but now everything's calm—too calm—so calm. I'm out of anger and frustration and confusion. I've got nothing roaring in my ears and pounding in my chest. All I've got left is this lingering weight in my heart and sting in my eyes.

My thumb finally presses down on my phone before bringing it to my ear. My lungs stutter with each inhale as

the phone rings and rings.

"Hello?"

The tears are warm as they stream down my cheeks.

"Mom?"

****

"Thank you for coming." I slam the passenger side door shut behind me.

"Always."

I can feel my mom's eyes. I've felt them since I opened the back door and chucked in my duffle bag and a few other things I was planning on taking home during spring break. I only had a few more days, and yet my mom's eyes are on me because I just couldn't wait.

She doesn't say anything else, though. Instead, she puts the car in drive. The radio is on low, but the silence between us is palpable. It turns my head into a dryer as all the stupid, meaningless things begin circling around and around. And…flop. And…flop. And…flop.

I dig the heels of my hands into my eyes. "It's so stupid."

"What?" my mom coos. "What's wrong?"

It takes an hour and a little more than thirty minutes out of the three-hour car ride home for the topic of Trent to finally become exhausted. Tears, snot, and reassurance all in an hour and thirty-seven minutes if I watched the clock correctly.

My face is still red but has been dry of tears since the hour mark. However, I feel the red-hot sting resurfacing because seven months of my life only took less than two hours to be summed up.

Seven months of my life shattered by two sentences.

****

"But why?" Layla's whine travels up the stairs.

"You know why." My mom hisses after hearing the same kind of whine spill from my sister's lips for the last few days.

"Can we at least get a cat?"

"No."

"*Please.*" Layla drags out the word.

"Enough!" My dad bellows this time, and I almost laugh, but it's my sister's dramatic sigh that makes my stomach jiggle.

"Fine." She huffs.

My parents turn the volume back up on the television. The actor's voices muffle Layla's heavy stomps up the wooden stairs. It's not long before her sock-covered feet scrape against the carpet in the doorway of my room. She stands there for a few seconds like she always does before she shuffles in closer.

Her oversized t-shirt and faded pajama pants get closer and closer until she flops down on the bed next to me.

"*Ugh.*" She sighs. "Your mattress is uncomfortable."

I turn my head, noting the way the thin blonde strands of her hair blend in with some of the flowers in my comforter. She makes sure her bangs are still separated down the middle.

The slow up and down movement of our chests counts the seconds. I guess, in a way, they always do.

I cast my gaze back on the ceiling. It doesn't take long for me to spot the glow-in-the-dark stars resting in the

corner above the door. I've always used those stars as my personal wishing well, but lately, I don't even know what to wish for.

"What an a**hole."

"Dad?" I choke on my salvia.

"No."

My body stills again. "Oh."

"Seriously, how the heck do you sleep on this?" She continues to wiggle around before settling on her side, facing me. A few minutes pass before she speaks again. "You know you have sixty-two freckles on the side of your face?"

My lips curve up to the side as I pass her a sideways glance.

"No, wait! Don't move." She uses her pointer finger to count as she quietly mouths the numbers. "It's sixty-seven—no! I forgot your forehead!"

My stomach jiggles as I laugh. The smile almost feels foreign to my cheeks, but it also feels good. It feels like home.

CHAPTER TWENTY-EIGHT: BACK TO BASICS

No matter how many times I've walked up and down these stairs the last few months, I still feel out of breath when I reach the top. It doesn't help that today I'm dreading doing the things I have scrawled out in my planner. It all weighs on me like my books in my backpack.

I almost don't see the figure sitting slouched beside my door because when my gaze was focused on my shoes, it was easy to place him as someone else sitting outside someone else's door—someone else's problem. Instead, I come to a dramatic halt only two doors away from my own. It's so dramatic it even makes the heel of my converse squeak against the graying white linoleum floors. It's almost too ironic that the color is practically identical to the one in the grocery store. It's even more ironic that this isn't the first time I've made that connection, but it is the first time I've made it ironically as opposed to sentimentally.

Even though my shoe squeaked, it takes Trent a few beats to finally look up—naturally—as if finally, unconsciously and subconsciously, feeling my stare.

"Oh, um." He shakes his head and sits up a little. "Hey."

"Hey—" I force myself to start walking again only because the sooner I start walking, the sooner I can reach

my door, and the sooner I can lock myself inside.

"I'm sorry," Trent says before trying to lift himself off the ground. "I know I shouldn't be here, but..." He huffs and slumps back down.

"How did you even get in here?"

He throws his head back to meet my gaze. "Made out with some girl in the elevator."

Why am I not in my dorm yet?

"I'm kidding. I'm kidding." He smirks down at his hands before his voice drops back down. "Lacie, I'm... kidding."

I twist around and grab my I.D. from my backpack.

"Wait...Can we...I wanted to talk."

"Now's not really good time."

"I know, but—wait."

"Trent."

He's looking up at me again with the hallway lights shining in the corners of his eyes.

"You're drunk."

"Yeah, I know, but...you watch movies. I drink, remember?"

"Yeah, okay." I go to push open the door. "That was before."

"Before what?"

I slide my I.D. through. It turns green.

"Before what? Lacie." He grabs my ankle but then slowly withdraws his hand like he knows he has no right because he really doesn't have a right. "Please, I know I'm not right, right now. I can't think right now, but please... I want to know—explain it to me."

I shouldn't have to. That's what I want to say. Because that's what I thought, it didn't need to be explained. It was automatic. Innate. Intrinsic.

"I don't know. I thought…" The green light faded a few seconds ago, but I still can't even look him in the eyes. I don't want to because maybe it is stupid and meaningless. "When I didn't want to think, I thought about you, and I thought…you had me."

"But I did, I mean, I do. I mean." Trent shakes his head. "We had each other."

"No, because for me, there was no one else. No one else before you. No one else I ever worried about. No one else mattered but *you*. I thought you finally saw me—you finally picked me, but even then…I still wasn't good enough."

"No, you are good. I swear this is all on me—"

"That's why it hurt. I know I'm good enough, I've always been good enough, but I want someone else not just to see me but to choose me out of everyone else in the room." I bite my lip because I'm sick of crying. I'm sick of this sinking feeling in my gut every time someone doesn't match up with the person I thought they were in my head. I have no business building them up, but they have no business boxing me in. "I guess I'll always be the girl that sits alone in the library. Pretty from across the room, but never good enough to get to know, but just because you're a coward doesn't mean I'm childish. Just because you're too embarrassed to own up to your feelings doesn't make mine any less valid."

There's the silence—finally—the silence I want, the silence I expect walking up the stairs, but now that it's here, I realize I still expect something else. That's my problem. I'm always expecting something else. Something different. Something hypothetical and irrational, and who am I kidding, magical and idiotic and stupid and, because it'll never be real or rational in the slightest, meaningless.

At least I got him to shut up—to stop looking up at me with those puppy dog eyes.

I slide my ID through and push down on the handle before it can even click. I shove my body into the door.

Don't do it. Don't do it.

But I do.

I pass a glance back.

Like I always do because I'm always expecting, not necessarily something better, but something different. Something I can possibly, hypothetically, irrationally, and magically hold on to.

Instead, all I see are slumped shoulders and a bowed head, like he knows he has no right because he has no right.

I let the door slam closed behind me. It doesn't necessarily feel good, but it at least feels final. Tangible. Definite. Something I can hold on to stop thinking about all the stupid, meaningless things.

"I'm sorry."

"What?" I shake my head. "I mean—I didn't realize you were in here."

Stephanie sits up on her bed. "I'm sorry."

"For what?" I drop my backpack on the floor next to my desk.

"I'm the one…I'm the one that let him in."

"Oh—it's fine." I plunk down in my desk chair, wanting that to be the truth.

"It's—I thought—I don't know."

"What?"

She picks her phone back up. "Nothing."

"Seriously, what?"

She lifts her eyes to meet mine but quickly darts them back down. "It's none of my business."

I laugh, even though it feels hollow. "Everything is your

business."

She almost smiles but stops herself by biting her lip. "I'm not trying to tell you what to do. It's your life. I just thought—no one is going to think you're stupid if you give him a second chance."

She's not wrong—a double negative—Layla's favorite—because there's no way in hell I want to admit that she's the opposite of left. When she says it like that, like it's easy, one little push of a button, one little word with three little syllables, for-give-ness, it all seems plausible. Tangible. Doable. This whole thing, me being sad and mad, him being confused and sad, and both of us being lonely and sad, all feels so stupid. It should be easy to just slap on a band-aid and start fresh.

But that's not the problem. It's fine she let him in the building because he's not the problem anymore. It's me. No one would think I'm stupid, but I will. I'd think I'm stupid. I feel so stupid because I did it again. I narrowed my worldview until all I saw was him and nothing else. I ignored all the little things that meant something, all red and blaring in my face, and latched on to all the stupid, meaningless things instead because they made me feel all warm and giddy and colorful.

"I don't know." Stephanie lays back down. "Relationships are hard. They suck, actually, and people suck sometimes, but nobody's perfect, and, I don't know, at least he keeps coming back. He keeps showing up—that at least...means something..."

Maybe he just feels stupid, too. Stupid and lonely.

Mostly stupid, I hope.

CHAPTER TWENTY-NINE: SIMMER DOWN

If only time could mimic steps. Sometimes I want time to walk alongside me. Other times I want it to run right past me.

It always does the opposite.

I've been back in my routine. Wake up, run, go to class, do homework, sleep, and repeat. If only I could run away these last few weeks of classes. Pound time away into the cement with my sneaker.

"Another run?" Stephanie's annual question of the day.

Today, I laugh and jog in place before closing the door behind me.

My ponytail swings back and forth along to beat echoing in my ears from my earbuds. I walk down to the center of campus as a warmup before beginning to run.

I run away from the assignments I have to do when I get back. I run away from the dread of other assignments due in the future. I run away from the dull routine of today. Most importantly, I run away from the slight sting in my chest that still burns every time I catch a glimpse of dirty blonde hair.

It was cold this morning, but now the sun is out and searing my skin. It doesn't take long for my underarms, the back of my neck, and under my nose to feel slicked with

sweat. I also have to alternate my phone between my hands whenever the sweat starts to build there.

All the pounding of my feet, heart, and blood comes to a stop when I glance up from my sneakers. The same way a flower stretches its petals to the sun or when two squirrels duel for the same nut.

He's standing with his group of friends.

My immediate reaction is to look down and run in the opposite direction. Instead, I take a deep breath. I square my shoulders and keep my gaze level with the boy who hurt me—the only one that matters.

If there's anything I've learned from being with Trent is that I'm allowed to take up space. I'm allowed to show my passion for the things I love. I'm allowed to exist in full volume even if no one else cares. I don't need to shrink myself to fit inside someone else's eyes, least of all a boy who only stares at me from across the room. The people who choose to sit down next to me are the only ones that matter.

The boys that duck behind Trent's head with shaking shoulders and whispers are hiding their insecurities behind their "tubas."

I nod to Trent as if I'm communicating all of this to him before turning on my heel, but old habits die hard. I watch him in my periphery. He drops his backpack on the ground and starts shrugging off his navy-blue sweatshirt.

"Dude." The snickers ensue. "What are you doing?"

I start jogging again but pass a glance back. I can't help it. Trent's still magnetic even in the muddled haze of hurt and clarity. Especially when I find those eyes are dead set on me as he takes off running. He even has the audacity to smile—for only a second—before resuming his game face.

Here I thought I was being all poetic.

F*ck philosophy and hypotheses and theories and analyses. No matter how many lines I draw and conclusions I make, I've never been able to make any sense of this. F*ck stupid boys, their pretty faces, and their ability to get stuck in my head and worm their way into my heart until every ventricle is knotted up and all my blood vessels shout their name. F*ck me for always trying so hard, or maybe not trying hard enough. F*ck me for romanticizing little things like eye contact and pen twirling. F*ck me for being a junkie for the adrenaline high of unrequited love. F*ck me for always searching for feelings and then catching feelings that always leave me burning my heart at the stake. F*ck it all.

"Wait!"

I didn't stretch enough for sprints, but my heartbeat is already ahead of my music. I can feel people glancing back as I pass them, but I keep pushing. I keep pounding. I keep praying the frayed shoelace comes undone and trips him—gashes and scrapes and blood.

"I like you too." The blood had rushed straight from my heart and right to my cheeks, but it didn't matter because he smiled at me—that rare, teeth showing, million-dollar smile.

"Lacie." Trent breathes. He finally manages to grip my elbow and turn me around to face him.

I rip my arm away, but that's the only thing I can manage to do in between sucking in deep breaths. Trent's chest heaves up and down as he attempts to do the same.

I taste blood when I swallow. That's how I know this will hurt tomorrow and not just physically.

Trent's lips part, but then a car beeps and jolts both of us back into reality. We both take a step towards the parked cars beside us, so we don't get hit by the car trying to

maneuver through the parking lot.

Trent's grey T-shirt has sweat stains and wrinkles, but the frayed shoelace is still intact. His hands are on his hips as he continues to breathe in through his chest before he walks the few steps over to the curb and plops down.

He digs his hands into his hair as he shakes his head. "I'm sorry...for chasing you." He looks up. "And for..." His head falls back down between his legs. "Everything."

Everything.

Everything that used to be crystal clear, warm, and fuzzy now makes my eyes squeeze shut and my head shake.

It's like scrubbing at a carpet stain. You scrub and scrub, but all it does is keep spreading. All it does is make everything worse.

Stephanie's words echo in my head. *"At least he keeps showing up."*

I need it to stop spreading.

My legs are thankful the second my butt hits the cement, but the world is quiet when I pull out my earbuds. The breeze that blows by only makes my skin feel hotter and messes up my hair even more.

Trent's head ping pongs between me and the license plate in front of him. His hands won't stop leaving red marks on his skin before his shoulders sag, and he ducks his head again.

The car in front of me rumbles as it starts up before it pulls out of the spot. Now everyone who walks by has a front-row seat to the two of us, somber, sweaty people sitting on the curb.

"They wouldn't stop pestering me," Trent says. "They were pestering me for weeks, and I hate—" He passes a glance my way. "I hate when people think they *know* me."

I tuck my knees into my chest and wrap my arms

around my legs.

"I know." Trent holds his hand up. "I know that is not an excuse, but I felt so boxed in, and I—I choked."

I shift my leg and nudge the four silver pebbles resting beside my shoe.

"But I'm sick of being that guy. The one who doesn't go for what he wants because he's too worried about what everyone else thinks."

I can feel his eyes on me, blinking back at me, but I keep my gaze on the pebbles.

"I've never been good at all this—opening up to people. But it was easy with you. You know me, while they only know what they want to hear..." Trent swivels his knees around to face me. "Lacie, I really am sorry."

"Sorry I heard, or—"

"No," he sputters.

"Because what if I wasn't there? What if I heard nothing? Does that change anything?"

"No—I mean, yes." He shoves his fingers back into his hair.

"How do I know you aren't just telling me what I want to hear? How do I know you aren't lying to me?" Because he would step back. He'd smile behind his hand. He'd look past me as if making sure no one else was around. As if I wasn't even standing there. I knew all along, but I ignored it because it felt like a stupid, meaningless thing compared to all of our stupid, meaningless things.

"Because—" His hands go flinging into the air as he searches for the right words, but then everything goes still again. Everything goes quiet again. His voice softens. "Because I may lie to them, I may even lie to myself, but I would never...I would never lie to you."

"Who said that was a bad thing?"

"Because I like to cuddle."
"I love when you talk science to me."
"I would never force you to do anything."

"Look, I…" Trent scrubs a hand down his face. "I know my credibility with words is shot right now, but I need you to know that I didn't mean what I said. I swear, I didn't mean it. And you don't deserve it—any of it."

The red car in front of him revs as it starts up and slowly backs up. You would assume the person driving would be careless with such a loud and obnoxious engine. Instead, they take their time. Their movements are slow and cautious as they back out of the spot. They leave us with an even wider view of both the parking lot and the world beyond—pale blue sky, wispy clouds, trees tops, and buildings.

I focus my gaze on Trent as I lay my head on my arms. "I…" I breathe in through my nose. "I forgive you."

Not because I want to, but because I need to. For the sake of all the assignments I can't concentrate on. For the sake of all the muscles I keep pulling in my legs. For the sake of slowly moving forward.

Trent lifts his head and stares back at me. We stay like that for a few seconds, drinking each other in. Every time my chest expands on an inhale, his contracts on an exhale.

More car doors slam and rumble as they startup. There are distant conversations and laughter. But I still can't bring myself to move.

"I miss you." Trent's voice is soft.

My gaze finds the pebbles on the ground again as my heart squeezes in my chest. I would love to wrap my fingers around it and squeeze out all the ache myself, but it remains there. I'm still scrubbing and scrubbing away.

Trent lifts his hand and scratches at his neck. Then his

jaw. Then he pulls at the muscles in his cheeks. "What can I do?" His eyes go burning again, burning into me. "What can I do to fix this?"

My tongue presses against the roof of my mouth as the word "nothing" almost falls from my lips. Almost. It doesn't though because it's too final.

I still can't let all this go. No matter how many times I scrub and wring out my heart, I still don't want there to be nothing.

So, I continue to sit there with my cheek pressed against my arms as the late afternoon sun shines down on us both.

"I don't know."

CHAPTER THIRTY: EVALUATION

It's been twelve months, two weeks, and three days since I last stopped in this very spot in aisle three. Three months ago, it might have nearly broken me, shattered me into a thousand little pieces someone would need to sweep away with one of those insanely long blue brooms that span the entire aisle. It probably would have taken one pass through, and I'd be gone like any other possible mess on aisle three.

Yet here I am, now nineteen, once again on the search for a can of peas. It was easy this time—almost too easy—taking the can up off the shelf and into my hands, and yet I still can't bring myself to walk away. I keep rolling and rolling it between my fingers. Eighty calories for half a cup of undrained peas. Sixty calories for half a cup of drained peas. Six grams of total sugars. Four grams of dietary fiber. Zero grams of total fat. Ingredients: peas, water, sugar, sea salt. I keep rolling and rolling, reading the same things over and over because I see him standing at the opposite end of the aisle. Not actually him. But him. The guy in the maroon employee polo and grey sweatpants.

And I see her.

My past self from one year ago, flushed cheeks and high ponytail.

I smile because she's smiling. I smile because I can't be mad at him. He's not the one who shattered my heart into a thousand little pieces. He's just the cute guy in the grocery store.

I should be happy I found my can of peas without getting smacked in the head, and yet my legs are frozen. I still feel smacked in the face. Even as carts squeak by and people maneuver around me because I know I'll never have a moment like that ever again. It's not necessarily a sad revelation, rather simple. Things are back to the way they should be—easy—too easy—at least in the trivial, mundane, everyday sense.

Here I am in aisle three on the verge of another mental breakdown, but the good kind, a fresh bucket of ice water and a clean slate. I'm no longer blinded by the big flat ceiling lights above my head. Unlike before, when I felt exposed like a fish under a lamp, the spotlight shifts. My shoulders slump back down as the crowd applauses in my head, applauses for the catharsis. I am shedding the weight that has settled in my chest these past few months and inhaling the life back into my body, the self I've been missing, the girl that was left in the shadows of a dorm building basement.

I look down at the can of peas in my hand, and I see it for what it is—a can of peas.

I look back up at the empty aisle and see it for what it is—aisle three.

I see it all for what it was—a fleetingly absurd moment in time.

I could never have known I'd be crying in the middle of a grocery store over a can of peas. Not the bad kind of cry that blurs lines and makes your chest hurt, but the good kind that brings clarity to your mind, refreshes your eyes,

and swells your heart because that's the beauty of it all. I could never have known, never could have guessed, and neither could he. That's why we daydream about meeting cute boys in the grocery store. We are always looking for hope in the corners of ordinary places.

A can of peas could be just a can of peas, but it also could be a key ingredient to one of your favorite pasta dishes that your mom makes, especially because it made it taste even better than the frozen bag. Vanilla cake mix could very well be your go-to flavor for almost everything because it never disappoints you like a boy in a dorm building basement. A grocery store can just be a grocery store, and most of the time, it is.

But there's a reason why I couldn't find that damn can of peas the first time. There's a reason why I was left panicking in aisle three for way too long. One second earlier, or one second later, and I might have missed everything.

Everything.

Yet there's also a reason as to why I found them so easily today.

Every step in and out of grocery store aisles is another step closer to things you don't even know yet, and that's why you keep walking.

No moment will ever be like it.

That's why I stare down at the can one last time.

Him.

A boy I had yet to officially meet.

Her.

Past me, who I'd love to step back into, only for a moment, even though I know, she'll never fit me the same like a shirt you find all the way in the back of your closet. You cling to it for the sake of memories knowing that if

you put it on, it doesn't look or feel the same as it once did, and it never will, and yet you keep it. You hold on to it for dear life, even as your fingers let go. Your mind never does. Your heart never does.

"I got the milk and the eggs, but I am not touching the parmesan cheese." Layla starts pushing the shopping cart down the aisle. The wheels squeak every so often.

"Okay, we'll go together." I grab a few more canned vegetables off the shelf before meeting her halfway and dropping them in the cart.

She goes to walk again but stops. "I think...I think I want to be a writer."

"Yeah?"

She stares at her hands for another beat. "Yeah, my English teacher thinks I can do it, and Dr. Gracie thinks I can do it."

"I think you can, too."

She finally turns her head and meets my gaze. "You think so?"

"Yeah."

She hums an affirmation and starts pushing the cart again. We head back towards the dairy products, passing the bakery section.

"I also think you're not a bad driver—anymore."

"Thanks, Lay."

She stops again. Her light blue Crocs don't even make a sound against the linoleum. "No one else calls me that."

"Do you not want me to?"

"No, I..." She shakes her head and starts walking again. "No, I like it."

I take a second to absorb her words before catching up with her. The dairy aisle is colder the further we stroll down.

"Hey, Lay."

"What?"

"No one's in the aisle."

She pauses before dashing to the front of the cart. "Do the thing! Do the thing!"

Layla jumps up on the end of the cart. I make sure she's holding on before I start running. I push the cart forward a few steps before I jump on, sending us both sailing and squealing down the rest of the aisle.

Stopping is usually the problem I know my mom, was always worried about when we were little, but for a few seconds, Layla is smiling, and it's the first time I smile— truly smile—in three months.

CHAPTER THIRTY-ONE: CONCLUSION

Three weeks later

I catch the door from the person in front of me before walking out of the science building. The laces of my black converse flop around as I take the three steps down to the cement pathway before I look up. I look up because I'm determined to not always cast my gaze on the pavement. I might as well start enjoying the scenery while I'm here— all the white oaks and dogwoods. The green grass is always cut to perfection. The pockets of black woodchips and bushes. A mix of both man and nature.

Today, my steps falter because I catch a bright green gaze instead of leaves.

I stop in my tracks right there on the pavement, but at least people also move around Trent as he stands on the edge of the grass. His notebook is poised in one hand as he pulls his pen out of his mouth.

My backpack strap almost slips off my shoulder while my arms tighten around the earth science textbook I have hugged to my chest. I slowly lift my right hand. I don't twist my wrist, and my fingertips don't move, but it's still some form of a greeting that Trent even reciprocates before we both continue walking in opposite directions.

More grass, more cement, and more trees.

This pattern repeats for a few days each week. It's

always the same time and only when I step out of that building. I could opt for a different exit. Maybe I even should.

Instead, I take the three steps down and out before my hand lifts. Sometimes I take the three steps and then four or five steps before we cross paths. Other times I barely get down the steps before Trent lifts his hand.

I always catch him in transit or as he swerves onto the pathway and falls into step with everyone else. I always catch him without even trying.

There's no box of cake mix to knock me on the shoulder or pen tapping to steal my attention. My eyes zoom right in the same way my legs always fall into step.

That tree is dogwood, and today those jeans are Trent's. Those shorts are Trent's. Those socks are Trent's.

I get it right enough times the hand lift becomes paired with a closed mouth "I'm-not-sure-if-I-should-smile-or-not-so-I'll-give-you-something-that-resembles-frog-lips." Thankfully, somehow, Trent mimics the expression. I like to believe he even looks funnier doing it.

Then one day, the pattern breaks.

Trent's a few steps and people ahead of me but still decides to hold the door when he sees we walk into the same building. I speed up my pace to catch the gesture.

"How are you?" The question seems rhetorical, but his smile is gentle.

"Good. You?"

The space between us widens as he heads for the stairs while my sneaker squeaks as I keep walking right.

"Good." He nods.

Then we keep going, only this time the smiles have changed. The pleasantries allow for more real smiles to break out across our lips when we happen to pass each

other by, and sometimes even more words leave our mouths if greetings come up.

"Hey." He nods.

"Hey." I nod back.

"Hi." I smile.

"Hi." He smiles back.

Zack has also popped up a few times, but that's nothing new. Zack may have been the one to hit me on the head with a box of cake mix, but on campus, I'm always playing Whack-a-Zack.

"Whazzup?" he whispers in my ear as he passes. He never waits for my reply. He keeps walking, never missing a stride. Sometimes he'll throw me a grin over his shoulder. Other times he'll twist his ball cap around and joke about Stephanie's whereabouts. Most times, he keeps talking as he walks backward.

"Buffalo chicken lasagna, be there or be square."

"Ice cream sandwich lasagna! I can save you a piece."

"Peas! Chicken pot pie lasagna. You know you want some."

Each time, I only like the pictures Zack posts of his creations, but that brings technology back into the midst.

Funny pictures and videos from Trent that occur at any time of day and in between random meets. Only LOLs and laughing emojis are thrown into the mix of dialogue, but nothing else.

It takes a few weeks before real conversation regrows in the space between us. Sometimes classes and homework come up. Other times he recommends I watch a film on Netflix. If I find the time, I'll watch the trailers before clicking away, but a visit home for a weekend forces me to watch one with my family.

I text him only to say the movie was as good as he said

but wasn't planning on the twenty-minute rant that ensues back and forth between us. There were no pauses in response time and even some caps about how the directors could have made some characters better, but overall nailed the conflict.

It felt like merging onto an interstate. The routine is familiar, but the territory is new—lane changes and speed limits are all unknown and questionable.

It takes Stephanie being present for one of Whack-a-Zack occasions that lunch gets involved. For a couple of days, Trent and Zack end up pulling chairs up to our table. I may still jokingly be called a pea, but Trent and Zack are the true pod.

Our conversations are carried mainly by the banter between Stephanie and Zack under the umbrella when it's nice outside. More of Zack's friends are added to the mix inside the student center because the rectangular tables are bigger.

The television show and school rants become an eight to twelve-person debate. When Megan sits beside me, we quietly listen to the conversation together. If Stephanie and I end up next to each other, we have side conversations. When I end up next to Savannah, I always end up laughing at all her remarks, whether they're snide or not. Sometimes I snort way too loud, but Trent always remains on the opposite side of the table.

"You did not steal one of my tomatoes," Stephanie demands.

"Oh, but I did." Zack sends her a slow wink, but that only gets him a nice cherry tomato in the eye.

At first, my gut twisted every time Trent and I would make random eye contact. Especially when that eye contact was paired with leftover laugh smiles. My heart would turn

to stone and sink down into my stomach.

The smiles are what I miss most. Every time I blink after we lock eyes, a little camera flash goes off and provides me with a snapshot from before. Every little moment, every conversation, seemed so effortless. I used to replay them in my head just to bask in the warmth.

Yet there's something about these new smiles. They are starting to feel more real.

They make the ones from a year ago seem dull and blurry. Distant and scripted. I can no longer color the memories like a paint by number. I can't trace my finger along every detail or outline before and after.

These smiles are less tentative. They don't end up hidden behind hands or ducked down to face the pavement. They are big and goofy and random. Nothing is hiding behind them. These smiles lead us to a little more than halfway through the semester.

The air is brisk. I can feel it in the tips of my fingers and in the tip of my nose, but the sky is way too blue to sit inside. The clouds are way too white and puffy, and the weather is way warmer than usual for this time of year.

I still can't tell the difference between low-level and medium-level clouds. I do know cumulus clouds are the cotton balls and cirrus clouds are the wisps. Both are stark against the bright blue sky and cover the sun. Every time the sun pokes out and saturates us in yellows and oranges, another cloud covers it and brings back the blues and greys.

Trent's on one end of the black metal table while I'm on the other. The umbrellas were put away a couple of days ago, so our notebooks and lunch leftovers are the only things lying between us.

I fling my hands around. "Every dystopia is the same. Like, everyone's either already fighting each other or

preparing for a fight, and there's no in-between."

"Exactly!" Trent throws his hand out between us. "It's very pessimistic, you know, and violent."

"Right? I hate to think humanity would cave in so fast, but I think it's because of natural resources. Once they're all used up, it's every man for themselves."

"I hate that, though." Trent scrubs a hand down his face as he leans forward in his seat. "I hate how that's the default for everything."

"Me too." I nod. "But what gets me is it can all be prevented now—like we all can try to prevent it now, and yet we don't."

"True, very true." Trent rubs his jaw. "Take Oreos, for example—I'm serious." He smiles while I sputter out a breath. "They keep creating new flavors. Birthday cake, mint—"

"Red velvet." I interrupt with a smile of my own.

Trent's eyes sparkle back at me as the sun pokes back out. "That's an exception."

My eyes roll. "Always."

"As I was saying…" Trent's smile doesn't disappear even though the sun does. The right collar of his black peacoat is flipped up, but he tugs at the collar of the red sweatshirt he has underneath. "They keep creating new flavors when everyone knows the original is the best—"

"But!" I hold my finger up.

"Fine. The vanilla ones come in a close second."

"What? No, heads or tails."

"Tails never fails." He sing-songs, but I narrow my eyes, making him sigh and halfheartedly throw up his hands. "Fine, truce."

I nod and straighten back up in my seat, but Trent seems to do the same.

"All I'm trying to say is you would think that an Oreo wouldn't need to be competing because in most cases, it already won the race—"

"Chocolate chip—"

"Most." He holds his finger up, trying but failing to keep a serious façade. "Most cases. But instead, like you said, it's every man for themselves, and that's especially true in the business world. My politics professor always said that if you don't adapt, you die, and now an Oreo is not only competing against other cookies, but it's also even competing against other Oreos!"

I'm smiling at both his enthusiasm but also at the idea of someone other than the wind overhearing us right now.

"Sorry." Trent's words are soft. "I'm distracting you." He gestures to the reading material we both have spread over the table.

"No, it's fine." I wave my hand, trying to remember where I left off, but all I see are the tiny black words. "Did you," I start but pause to finish my internal debate—to ask or not to ask—before I decide to go for it because we've done this before. There's no need for qualms. Time is unapologetic. "Did you ever end up switching your major?"

"I did. Special education with a minor in physical education." He leans forward, his shoulders shadowing the lined pages of his notebook. "It's a lot of reading, and I'm doubling up on classes to catch up to maintain my scholarship, so it's a lot, but I'm happy cause I finally feel like I'm not only doing something for me but also…for kids."

"Good." I push my hair out of my face and tighten my grip on my pencil before glancing back up. A smile tugs at my lips, and Trent mirrors it. I lean my head on my hand

as we both look back down.

The wind rustles our papers and trash, but we both steady our things before focusing back on our schoolwork. I don't know about Trent, but I go back to my high-pressure and low-pressure systems.

Trent could be dealing with a high-pressure system with the way he starts chewing his sweatshirt string. Then again, low-pressure systems can be just as heavy, if not more so, because the air rises, expands, cools, and condenses into clouds, leading to rain.

Trent's chair scrapes against the cement as he scoots up further in his seat. The inside of his right sneaker aligns with the inside of my right boot.

"Ay! Look who it is!" Zack pulls back the chair on my right. "Would you believe that I, Zachary James Schmidt the third, got the last chocolate milk?" He starts shaking the bottle up as the chair on my left gets scraped back.

"I want to punch my professor in the face." Stephanie huffs as she plops down with her light blue backpack on her lap.

"I told you not to take his class again," I say.

"I know, but I couldn't help it. I'm a sucker for familiarity." She pulls out her laptop.

I catch Trent's gaze, only for a split second, not even, before quickly looking away.

"Way to ditch us, hoe bag." Savannah whacks the back of Stephanie's head.

"Hey!" She whines and rubs her curls in response.

Megan sends me a wave as she and Savannah lift some black metal chairs from a nearby table and bring them over.

"Wait, what are you doing?" Savannah says before making Megan squeal because she pulls her down on her lap. Megan's hair is back to chin length, but the ends are

dyed neon green, and Savannah buries her face in them. "We're not being productive right now, no way, no how."

Megan turns her head ever so slightly to whisper, "but I really need to read."

"And you will." Savannah secures her arms around her, backpack and all. "Later."

Meanwhile, Zack smirks at Stephanie over his chocolate milk. He takes a second to wiggle his eyebrows at me when he catches me looking. Stephanie only rolls her eyes.

"Stop looking at me like that, Zack Attack."

"Don't be jealous, Steph-a-knees." He breathes when he finally brings the milk back down.

"I'm not." She sing-songs as she starts typing away on her laptop.

I pass a glance back down at the papers in front of me while Zack leans down in my periphery.

"She's jealous because I got the last chocolate milk."

"Nobody cares." She deadpans.

Zack continues to grin like the fool he is before his head gets whacked, making his backward baseball cap fly forward off his head

"We were supposed to run lines." Bellamy glares at him as she yanks on a chair from another table. I also see red hair behind her as Sam brings over a chair.

The circular metal table is small to begin with, but now it looks even smaller with all the different people and chairs and jackets and backpacks squished and squeezed and tilted around it.

"Sorry." He shrugs. "I needed my chocolate milk and my peas." He winks at me.

Megan's digging around in her bag beside Trent. "Do any of y'all have a pen? I let some ding-dong borrow mine last class."

Stephanie and Savannah share a look before their eyes dart to Megan.

"Y'all!"

Megan stops rustling and looks back up as if she's going to say something, but her glare does all the talking.

"Y'all?" Bellamy drawls. "Y'all wait until I round up all the church mamas and get the town to shun you into the next century witch hunt."

Everyone blinks back at her for a beat before Savannah laughs and hugs Megan closer. "I think you've finally found your witch cult. High time to start cursing some men."

Trent and I lock eyes. The sun stretches back out from the clouds, warming the tops of my cheeks and the top of my head. I look down at my reading but glance back up. Trent's hair is shorter on the sides and on top, shorter than it was when we met, shorter than last week. I don't like it.

"Your hair." I blurt when the people around us seem to be sucked back into their worlds.

He reaches up and rubs his head. "I know."

I remember his foot is still pressed against mine. We're back in our world—just him and me across the table.

I blink and blink as everything rolls through my mind like a movie trailer. Trent stares back at me as if he can see it too.

His laugh lines. His lopsided smiles. His quiet chuckles. His cotton sweatshirts wrapped around me from behind, or his t-shirt fisted in my hand. His fingers slowly tracing down my arm to my wrist. His hands wrapped around mine, palm to palm, to brace the cold. His lips nudging against mine turned to smiles nudging smiles. His legs taking the first step back on the pavement, patiently waiting for me to do the same. His eyes staring back at me, communicating with me, without saying a single word.

Clear, charge to three-hundred, *boom splat*, and shock delivered.

Boom, splat.

Everything.

We stare back at each other, almost like a challenge at first. I'm the first to break, and Trent follows, but I glance back up before I can help it.

He flashes in and out. His jacket morphs into a maroon polo. His hair grows up into a spike and back down. His eyes burn the same no matter what.

"I'm Trent." A huff of air and crinkled, smiling eyes. *"And I guess it's right there."*

It's him, but it's not him.

It's familiar, but it's not.

It still hurts, maybe it always will, but it's also healing.

"So." He nods to the papers in front of me. "How does snow form?"

"Well." I pause for dramatic effect. "If you're dying to know…"

He slowly, tentatively starts to smile.

I slowly, tentatively do the same.

It's him and me, but not him and me, rather it's him. It's me. Oil and water. Oxygen and Carbon dioxide. Vanilla and red velvet. Completely separate entities that can stand on their own, and yet there we were across from each other in an aisle. Here we are across from each other at the same table. His eyes are burning into mine, so different, yet still so the same.

There will be no restart or rewinds.

It's not a promise of a second chance.

But I don't move my foot away, and for now, that's enough.

TO MY READERS

Thank you so much for taking the time to read this story! If you found me in 2014 when I wrote my first story based on a weird dream I had about painting backdrops in a school theater in my bra, thank you. If you found me in 2015 when I first wrote *this* story based solely on the idea of a grocery store meet-cute by getting hit in the head by a box of cake mix, thank you. If you followed me chapter by chapter, or read once it was completed, thank you. If you loved the original version of this story, thank you. If you reread this story when I edited it back in 2019 and completely changed the ending, thank you. If you've been here with me since the beginning, or you found me along the way, thank you. If you ever took the time to read my words on a screen, thank you. If you ever voted, commented, or just silently read your way to the next chapter, thank you. If you are reading this right now, thank you. Thank you, thank you, thank you!

Over the years, I feel like I've grown up with and alongside you. Thank you for always sending love, happiness, and kindness my way! I'm forever sending it right back! I would not have the confidence to do this without you!

I love you! <3

Thank you so much for reading!

I'll see you in my next one!

XOXO,
lalalalawriting

ACKNOWLEDGEMENTS

Mom, thank you for being my number one fan. Your love is unconditional and powerful. I feel it with every fiber of my being. I would not be the person I am today without you. Dad, thank you for always calling me a nerd to my face, but secretly praising me behind my back. I love you. My sisters, thank you for being my best friends. You each make up a chamber of my heart and without you mine would not beat. My love and support for you is as endless as your love and support for me.

My work family, especially my M&Ms, thank you for being my biggest cheerleaders, for adopting and bragging about me as if I were your own while also letting me pretend like your kids are mine. I love you, guys.

My forever friend, you're the reason I believe in fate. I feel like we met in a past life and will continue to do so forever. Thank you for supporting me since day one.

My editor, Alex, I'm so glad I found you. Thank you for all your help. I had so much fun working with you.

My younger self, who decided to start writing her daydreams down so she can read them for fun later, thank you for always doing this for you, for never giving up, and for writing because after all these years it's now our oxygen, and this is how we breathe.

Lastly, once again, my readers—you right now if you are reading this—thank you with all my heart. I am nothing without you.

@lalalalawriting

just a girl who loves to write

lalalalawriting is a 2021 Watty Award Winner who has been writing teen fiction novels on Wattpad since she was fourteen years old where she has amassed over half a million reads and over five thousand followers. Offline, she goes by the name Julianna and has a B.A. in English with a concentration in writing and minor in sociology. She is a hopeless romantic bookworm, realist writer, and tea enthusiast who daydreams too much and re-watches her favorite movies over and over again.

IF YOU ENJOYED, PLEASE DON'T FORGET TO LEAVE A REVIEW!

lalalalawriting:
lɑːˈlɑːlɑːˈlɑː/ˈrīdiNG/
A girl who loves to write

Potentially You & Me

LALALALAWRITING